# HEARTS & HAUNTS

*Confessions of a Closet Medium, Book 3*

# NYX HALLIWELL

Beach
Path
Publishing

Hearts & Haunts, Confessions of a Closet Medium, Book 3

© 2021 Nyx Halliwell

ISBN: 978-1-948686-40-2

Cover Art by EDH Graphics

Formatting by Beach Path Publishing, LLC

Editing by Beth Neal, Patricia Essex

Please Note

The Nottingham Hotel stood majestic and ominous against the cloudy sky. Three stories of turn-of-the-century Gothic architecture imposed itself above me as I stood in the parking lot with Persephone floating lazily at my side. A drizzle had begun, the chill of the morning trying to sneak under my coat.

"Tallulah was born here in nineteen twenty," my guardian angel tells me. "The Roaring Twenties. The economy was booming, and they were filled with too much champagne and plenty of debaucheries."

"Are you speaking from experience?" I tease.

Rosie is gathering boxes from the back of our van, her dark hair blowing in the wind. She snugs the belt of her raincoat tighter and places a stack on the cart provided by the hotel. I need to help her, but I'm sure by the look on Persephone's face the crash course in history isn't over.

"Her father, Emanuele, built the hotel," she continues. "Everything was great until he died while Tallulah was still young, and she had to take care of her mother. It fell into disrepair, yet it was the only thing they had. After World War

II, they reopened, but it was slow going. Times were still hard. On any given month, they only had a few guests. Eventually, they rebranded and called it a health resort to help men returning from the war deal with their mental issues."

Another van pulls in. We're getting ready for the Hearts Forever Bridal Fair taking place over the next four days. Wedding suppliers from all over the state will be coming today to set up booths, and tonight kicks off with a wedding gown runway event.

I hardly want to be standing here, appearing to be talking to myself, since no one can see Persephone, but I don't have much choice. "I know you want me to help this ghost." I turn slightly, so the folks in the van can't see me staring at the hotel and talking to air. "But I do have a bridal fair to attend."

"Mary Mae, Tallulah's mother, passed in 1950. Tallulah died at age eighty-four. She never married, and unfortunately, she's never crossed over. She has haunted the subsequent owners and guests ever since. Trust me. If you don't get this ghost to cross to the other side, your bridal fair is going to be a hot mess."

Rosie wheels the cart around the side of the van. "Can I get a little help here?"

I leave Persephone and push the cart toward the back entrance. Along with all the suppliers, brides from the tri-state area will also be attending. Some will stay in the hotel, along with the various wedding consultants and reps from the bridal supply businesses.

Blue skies are predicted for later in the week, but at the moment, I'm heading into a haunted mansion with a rainstorm about to break.

"Everything okay?" Rosie asks, glancing up at the imposing structure. I follow her gaze and notice a shimmering white presence in the far top floor window.

"Of course," I lie. "Couldn't be better."

A medium sized man with a messy goatee and scuffed up shoes props open the service door and lends a hand, wiggling the cart over the threshold and inside. "Welcome, welcome." He's beaming from ear to ear, and I imagine he's quite happy with the fact the fair had to be moved here at the last minute. He'll be making a chunk of change from this, considering those who'll be staying here this weekend and attending the event. "My name is Baldwin. Please let me know if you need anything."

I push the heavy cart down a long hall with antique sconces that give off a yellowy glow. We pass a large atrium and courtyard with planters and concrete statues of angels, fairies and various animals. The coordinator of the fair, Victoria Jenkins, in a smart black blazer, white shirt, and black skirt, peers over dark-framed reading glasses and opens her metal document holder. "Name?"

"I'm Ava Fantome, and this is Rosie Rodriguez. We're Enchanted Events."

I'm sure Victoria remembers me from previous bridal fairs, but I understand her need for coordination. I recall her Type A personality, and respect it. It's precisely what's required for an event this size.

She shuffles efficiently through the papers, finds the one with our info, and slides it under the metal clip on the top of the holder. With a silver pen, she checks several boxes, then hands Rosie a packet of information. Slipping our form back inside, she motions down another hall to a pair of open doors. "Vendors are to set up in the ballroom. Please have your booth ready and available for inspection by three. The runway event begins at seven sharp, and since you'll be participating with a selection of your gowns, Miss Fantome, you and your models will be expected to be in the dressing area located behind the stage by five."

Not only have I expanded Aunt Willa's business, I now

have my own line of bridal gowns that I'm excited to unveil tonight. Rosie takes the packet from Victoria, and I heave on the cart to get it rolling again. "Thank you very much," I call over my shoulder. She's already moved on to the next vendor in line.

Rosie rubs her tummy, and I see how tired she looks. "You up for this?"

She nods. "I never had this much morning sickness with Mike. I'm not used to feeling so out of sorts."

We enter the grand ballroom. It's larger than I imagined, even after seeing the size of the hotel.

This room is easily three times bigger than the Thorn-hollow Country Club, where most local events are held. Previously, Hearts Forever was planned to take place at one of the local school's gyms, but when the roof started leaking two days ago, there was no way to make that happen. The Nottingham Hotel, and its grand estate that covers several acres of rolling hills, a lake, and an old horse barn and paddock, is the largest building in the county that could be rented on such short notice.

Unfortunately—at least for me—it comes with a healthy dose of spirits.

Rosie removes a map with the layout and points to a section along the far wall. Tape on the floor denotes each vendor's area for their tables and displays. We move to the one marked for us. As we begin unloading the boxes, I notice a man wheeling in a covered hanger with the words Southern Bride written in fancy script on it.

My pulse skips, and I look around for my former boss. I knew they'd be here, but I hadn't thought about seeing Darinda since I quit my job in Atlanta to move home and take over Aunt Willa's business.

The dark-haired man is my height and very thin, but dressed to the nines in a suit and bow tie. He bosses around a young woman who looks harried and cuts him a few nasty glares when he's not looking.

Salvatore Luxton was my underling and a pain in my backside for many years at the sizable company. He stands and directs his helper with a pretentious air, and my heart goes out to her. I'm sure he hasn't changed one bit, and before I can turn away, he catches me watching them.

He claps his hands together once and calls out, "Avalon!"

"Great," I moan under my breath.

Sal promptly sashays over and tries to grab my hand. I pick up a large book filled with invitation samples and hold it in front of me like a shield. "Hi, Sal. How's it going?"

His dark eyes laugh at me, knowing exactly what I'm doing to keep him at a distance. "This is absolutely a disaster," he says, "holding such a classy event in this old hotel. Why that little dive, Thornhollow, right down the road? It doesn't even have a decent restaurant. I can't imagine staying three nights in this place."

He glances at the towering ceiling, sniffing at the chandeliers. Several are missing bulbs, and even more have errant holes where the elaborate glass teardrops should hang.

"I rather like it." I'd say anything to contradict him, and I call up what the brochure said. "This place has a lot of character. It was once as grand as the Biltmore estate up north, and people came from all around to vacation here."

My argument falls flat when the chandelier above us flickers and goes out.

Regardless, I'm undaunted. "By the way, Thornhollow is my hometown." I'm sure he knows this. "There's a great restaurant called The Beehive Diner, though it's probably beneath your standards."

Sal frowns up at the light that has thrown us into a shadow. "Yes, well, thank you for leaving Southern Bride." He leans in as if he has a secret to tell. "I'm second in charge now, having been promoted to your former position."

He's all smiles, and I feel Rosie hovering behind me. Her shoulder touches mine, a show of solidarity, "Ava's talents were certainly wasted there. Have you seen the announcement?"

He feigns confusion. "Are you finally getting married?"

A sore spot in the wedding biz—not, in fact, *being* married.

Rosie brushes that off. "She has a line of wedding gowns coming out, and she's doing the big reveal tonight!"

Sal straightens. He peers at the cart and our boxes. "Where are they?"

"You'll get to see them on the runway, like everyone else." I turn away to let him know I'm done with this conversation. There's no way I'm allowing him to have an early peek.

He takes the hint, says a churlish goodbye, and returns to his striped area. As Rosie and I set up our double tables and shake out the cloths to cover them, she once again grabs her belly and takes off, green around the gills.

I hope she knows where the restroom is. I debate following her to make sure she's okay. The next few days may be quite interesting for both of us if her hormones don't settle down.

As I continue to set up the display of our services, the ghosts of the past vie for my attention, flickering in and out like a TV with poor reception. Most are caught in time loops, replaying events that happened many years ago. Some dance and laugh; others appear heartbroken and down on their luck.

It's not hard for me to imagine what it was like in the beginning, when the estate was intact, and the rich and famous attended parties, events, and weddings here. I bet it was amazing when decorated for Christmas, and I'm sure people came to get away from it all at times. They spent summer vacations dipping in the pond, took long walks on the beautiful grounds, and watched the changing of the leaves in the fall.

Seeing the original architecture, especially in the ballroom, inspires me. I've been working on a second line of dresses, based on templates from this period, to give modernday brides a classy, sleek option. I think about the one I designed at Christmas for myself, and how I've been dreaming of marrying the guy I'm in love with.

Thinking of Logan and his sexy smile puts me in a much better mood. At least until Victoria announces she has to switch several vendor locations. She's been schmoozing reps, and the next thing I know, Sal and his young assistant are next to Rosie and me.

When Rosie finally returns, she makes a face at the new arrangements, and I have to hold my tongue as I overhear Sal say, "Guess we're next to each other. Won't this be fun?"

I ignore him, and Rosie follows my lead. Once again, I check to make sure she's feeling okay, and she assures me she's fine. We unpack the last of our items and begin dressing the mannequin we brought. This dress has been in the front window of The Wedding Chapel already. Rosie and I named it the Bellamy. She helps me adjust the waist as the skirt cascades elegantly to the floor.

Sal stops what he's doing and looks it over. "Is that one of yours?"

I shift a stack of the thin but eye-catching catalog of my designs that Gloria, Rosie, and I have put together. The woman who sews the gowns has been an integral part of getting me ready for this debut tonight, and we're all very proud of the photoshoot.

I step in front of them so he won't see it. "Yes, it is. I've already taken orders for it, and I suspect it will be a bestseller."

Mama and her best friend, Queenie, show up in a cloud of Estee Lauder and Southern manners. I hug them, my attention dragged from Sal. They go on and on about the building, the booths, and how proud Aunt Willa would be of me right now. Really, it's such a show, I almost flush with embarrassment, but honestly, it feels nice, too.

We put the finishing touches on everything, and, as if the hotel is cooperating, the chandelier above flickers back to life. Rosie claps her hands, and I send up a thank you to Persephone, because I have a sudden intuitive hit that she played a part in it. As the four of us chat about going to get lunch, I hear Sal's assistant say, "They're beautiful. I bet Darinda will want to carry them."

Sal snickers. "Don't be ridiculous. They're amateurish at best."

With horror, I realize he's nicked a catalog and seen everything. Steaming, I'm about to turn on my heel and go off on him, but before I can, Rosie makes a funny noise. I glance over to see her face contort.

*Oh no.*

None of us are fast enough, and Rosie knocks into the table in an effort to run from the booth. Her hands fly out to stop the catalogs from sliding off, her foot catches the table leg, and as she attempts not to fall, she vomits all over the gown.

※ 2 ※

L uckily, Rosie had little in her stomach, thanks to her
earlier visit to the restroom.

As she rushes off, Queenie and Mama help me get the
dress off the mannequin, then Queenie leaves to take it to the
local dry cleaners.

The rest of the day passes with less excitement, and I
avoid Sal at all costs. Between the two booths, we have
enough archways and flowing swatches of material to keep us
from seeing each other.

While Southern Bride has very specific and elegant décor
that makes you feel like you're in one of their stores, mine is
more on the cost-efficient side. Rosie and I drape sections of
white and pink satin over the handmade wooden archways
Logan built for us. We've brought containers filled with some
of Aunt Willa's favorite plants to make more of a garden
atmosphere, and I'm quite satisfied with the results when
Victoria comes around at three to inspect.

She reminds me of an Army sergeant with her tape
measure and clipboard. A flurry of notes are made, suggested

changes offered, and she refers to numbered guidelines in the packets of information we received.

Southern Bride has spilled out over their allotted space, and she reprimands Sal. Everything at ours is according to code. We pass without any further action on our part, and Rosie and I breathe a sigh of relief.

Queenie texts to let me know the cleaners have assured her the Bellamy will be back in perfect condition by morning. That still leaves me short for tonight's runway show.

I hastily call Gloria and ask about the progress on my Christmas dress. I still don't have a name for the sleek flapper design, but she assures me she can tack the last few seams and rush it to the hotel before the event.

Now all I need is a name. Persephone bops in as I'm hanging a garment bag on our rolling rack. "Let's go check the west wing."

Rosie has wandered off to inspect the other vendors and chat with them. Since we offer a full package service, we like to be on friendly terms with area bakeries, florists, dance instructors, vacation planners, photographers, and anyone else associated with weddings. Mama has hailed a friend and is gossiping near the open French doors, laughing and waving at others as if she's the hostess.

I back into the booth and turn away from prying eyes, pretending to fiddle with a plant. "I can't go ghost hunting right now. Tallulah will have to wait."

"Sorry? Were you speaking to me?"

I whirl to find Victoria standing inside the entrance. "Oh, hi. I didn't know you were there." No sense in admitting I'm talking to myself.

"Your display is cute. Very...*down home*." Her voice drops as she says the last word and has a tone to it. She fiddles with the corner of one of the catalogs. "On Saturday, we're having guest speakers in the conference room for a variety of seminars."

Persephone has left. My phone on the table lights up with a text from Logan. I pocket it and stand behind the table. "I saw that on the itinerary. I'm sure many of the brides will attend just for that. It looks like you have a good lineup of experts."

"We did. Unfortunately, Karen Melrose had to bow out. She has a sore throat and lost her voice. I'd like you to fill in, perhaps talk about finding the perfect dress."

"Me?"

I start to add, *what would I know about that*, but stop myself. The businesswoman in me realizes this is an excellent chance to spread the word about my new line. My inner introvert, however, screams *no*. Standing in front of groups of people to do an impromptu speech is right up there with my worst nightmare. "Surely, you could ask someone else."

Victoria gives me a tight smile. "I was hoping to give a local business the first opportunity. Guess I'll have to offer the slot to one of the bigger venues from Atlanta."

Her gaze flicks to the left, and I know she's talking about Sal.

The words are out of my mouth before I can call them back. "I'd love to do it."

Her smile turns triumphant.

Around four-thirty, one of my models, Penn Reed, shows up to get ready. With her is her younger sister, Jenn. They ooh and aah over the booth, chat with Rosie and Mama, then Penn pulls me aside. "Hope you don't mind me bringing my sister. I thought you could use her help."

I eye Jenn, mentally sizing up which dress might look good on her frame. She and Rosie laugh over something Rosie says, and I wonder what Jenn looks like under her camouflage pants, motorcycle boots, and the oversize tunic she wears beneath a leather jacket.

She appears to have an equal amount of piercings as her sister, and I see a tattoo on the side of her neck below her left ear. They're both unique, and since Rosie's morning sickness could interfere with how many times I can parade her out, I figure I better take all the assistance I can get. "Actually that'd be great."

Penn glances at her sister and lowers her voice. "I was hoping I could ask a favor. Jenn is preggers, and she's not getting married until June."

Penn is nothing if not direct.

"Okay..." I nod, wondering where this is going.

"Her fiancé is in the Army and won't be home beforehand. She'll be eight months along. Do you think you can design an expandable dress?"

Mama has busied herself on her phone, leaving the four of us. Rosie and Jenn have quit talking, and I see they've overheard. Jenn gives me a sweet, shy smile. "I have my heart set on a white one, and Penn said you're the best."

Rosie and I exchange a look, and at that moment, Gloria hustles up to our booth.

We greet the seamstress, and she hands Rosie a garment bag that contains my unnamed dress. Introductions are made, and I worry my bottom lip, considering the sisters' request. From what I know about Penn, the two have had a rough life, and they've still managed to stay kind and considerate. I sense Aunt Willa on my right shoulder and swear I hear her whisper, "Do it, Ava. You won't be sorry."

My mind is already at work on how to make it. My gaze trails to the swooping fabric we created our booth out of, and an idea strikes. "If nothing else, I'll wrap you in a silk toga and make you a goddess for the day."

Jenn claps her hands and squeals, bouncing on her toes.

Penn smiles at me with deep appreciation. They leave to visit the other booths before going backstage to get ready, and Rosie shakes her head. "You're such a pushover."

I shrug, Gloria laughs, then I spot an orange tail disappearing under the cloth of the table.

"Is that your cat?" Gloria asks.

I peel up the edge to find Tabby starring back at me. She meows, and I briefly consider wringing her neck. "What are you doing here?"

The cat doesn't respond with any more than a blink of her eyes. I haul her out and lift her in my arms. Good Lord, she's getting fat. "She must have hitchhiked in the van."

Rosie makes a face and skedaddles for the door, another round of sickness hitting her. Hers lasts all day.

Gloria scratches Tabby under her chin and watches Rosie's fleeing back. "Do you think it wise to put her in a gown and send her out on stage?"

"I don't have a lot of choice at this point. Each designer is supposed to display five. I only have three models at the moment, unless I don one myself."

"That would be exciting."

Not exactly the term I'd use for it. "I need to stay backstage to make sure it all goes smoothly."

"I can stay. Perhaps do their hair and assist them getting in and out of the creations."

A male ghost appears over her shoulder suddenly and startles me. Tabby hisses and Gloria retrieves her hand, afraid of the cat.

Instantaneously, he vanishes, like one of the random ghosts floating around the ballroom. They continue to flicker in and out due to a lack of energy, and I know the hotel has a long history of being haunted.

Persephone warned me at Christmas that Gloria has a ghost problem. He may be the one.

Tabby leaps from my hold and scrambles away. I hear a baby's laugh echo in the booth, and I spin to look, but there's no one there—human or ghost.

The next few days are going to be interesting. I smile at Gloria. "I'm pretty sure I can use all the help I can get."

࿔ 3 ࿐

Just before seven, Logan Cross III, leans over to kiss my cheek. "Break a leg," he says.

I smooth a lock of his sandy blond hair off his forehead. "Thanks. I'm nervous."

Tabby hops on a nearby table where Penn and Jenn are putting their hair up in front of a large, rectangular mirror, with Gloria's assistance. A few of the Southern Bride crew, as well as models from two other wedding vendors, are applying makeup and donning accessories. Rosie is in our assigned fitting room, and she'll be the first to walk out in one of my designs.

"You have nothing to be nervous about." Logan squeezes my hands. The diamond tennis bracelet he gave me at Christmas reflects the overhead lights and reminds me how much he loves me. "You're gonna knock 'em dead."

He winks, and I make a face. He knows I can see ghosts, and although it makes him uncomfortable, that doesn't stop him from taking every chance he can to tease me about it.

I peek out the side curtain and notice there are as many ghosts milling around as there are real people.

I wish I could disappear into his pretty blue eyes at the moment and forget those in physical form as well as in spirit. "There are enough deceased here already," I tell him. "They don't need me adding to the population."

Sal and his assistant are busy accessorizing one of their models. Baldwin and Victoria are on stage, requesting that the crowd take their seats. I estimate close to two hundred, and it's standing room only.

Which only makes my nervous stomach flip-flop like a dying fish on land.

Gloria hustles past, winking at me and saying hello to Logan. "It's almost time!"

Logan gives me another squeeze and departs. In his wake, Darinda, the executive manager of Southern Bride, strides in. We haven't seen each other in months, but her eyes light up, and she hugs me. "Ava, so good to see you. I hear you're doing well."

She's a striking brunette with chocolate brown eyes. In her heels, she's at least six inches taller than me.

The crowd out front has settled, and it's not hard to hear Sal snicker at the compliment. I'm growing tired of his attitude, but I keep my gracious face on and thank my former mentor. "It's hard for me to believe I've come this far in such a short time."

She winks. "Following your dreams can do that for you."

Patting my arm, she wishes me luck as goes to help Sal. Rosie exits the dressing room, her expression worried. She rushes over. "We have a problem."

Her hair is swept up on one side with a pearl and rhinestone comb. Her eyes are professionally done, and she looks quite the femme fatale.

"Are you too sick?"

She shakes her head. "It's not me." She shifts to show me

the underside of the satin below her left breast. "There's dirt on the material."

Automatically, I attempt to brush it off. The gowns were stored individually in their garment bags and haven't been out of them since we had them cleaned for the show. "How did that happen?"

"No idea. There's something else."

Penn and Jenn have risen from the makeup table and joined us. They each try their hand at wiping the stain from the dress, but it does no good. It appears as though someone deliberately rubbed it into the white fabric.

I check the rest of the dress, but don't see any other damage. "What?"

Rosie glances around the area. "The shoes. I can't find any of the boxes."

We were instructed to set up earlier, and did so, leaving the dresses, shoes, and accessories back here in our appointed spots. "Are you kidding? Someone stole them?"

Sal moseys over at that moment, finger and thumb on his chin as he eyes Rosie's dress. "Something wrong?"

I lower my voice and indicate the stain. "Did you have something to do with this?"

His fake surprise suggests that he did, but of course, he denies it. "You think I'd bother to sabotage your amateurish line?"

Darinda is lining up their models in a staggered fashion. "Christine get over here."

Music kicks off with a modern pop beat, and the lights beyond the stage dim. One of the other wedding gown reps begins arguing with her over who's going first.

I see a look enter my former boss's eyes that's familiar. She places hands on her hips and gets in the woman's face, causing the gal to step back. At that moment, Victoria intervenes and tells Darinda she'll be last.

Darinda argues as the other vendor motions at her models to line up. I canvass the area, looking for the shoes.

"I don't put anything past you," I mutter just loud enough for Sal to hear.

Victoria wins the battle with Darinda then steps over to us. "What's wrong?"

Sal rolls his eyes and strides back to the woman he was dressing. "You shouldn't invite amateurs to a professional gig like this," he tosses over his shoulder at her.

Infuriated, I'm more determined than ever to show off my gowns. I give Victoria a big smile. "Everything is perfect."

Two tiny creases appear in her forehead as her brows bunch together. She glances at Sal, nods, and returns to her podium on stage. She and Baldwin take turns announcing the models and the names of the dresses.

"What are we going to do?" Rosie asks, panic in her voice.

Tabby yawns and begins cleaning a paw. I grab her and hand her to Rosie. Both cat and assistant stare at me with startled expressions. "Your new accessory," I say. "She's covering the spot."

As Penn and Jenn check out the fact that the feline is indeed hiding the stain, I point a finger in Tabby's face. "Cooperate or else."

Rosie is still panicked. "What about the shoes?"

All the gowns are floor-length and no one will see them anyway. "You're going barefoot."

Once the first vendor is winding down, I put the finishing touches on Penn and Jenn, then line them up with Rosie. I plan to send her out first, then the sisters while she's changing into the next dress that's waiting for her in the fitting room.

As the three stand in position, the lights and music echoing through the ballroom and backstage, the sisters take turns making over Tabby. My ancestor—who lives in the shape-shifting form of a cat—eats it up.

When Victoria announces the Enchanted wedding gown line, featuring Rosie and a dress I've named the 'Ella' since it is reminiscent of a fairytale, I hold my breath. This is it...the moment I've been waiting for.

I hear the crowd react. "Look at the cat!"

"Why does she have that?"

"Isn't he adorable?"

Persephone appears next to my elbow. "Better get out there and salvage this before it goes downhill. Tabitha will shapeshift into her human form and knock out whoever called her a boy. If that happens, you'll sink like the Titanic."

My guardian angel is often unreliable and unhelpful, but my intuition agrees. However, that would mean going on stage in front of the huge crowd.

"You sent that cat out there?" Sal sneers. "How absolutely unprofessional. A new low, even for you."

"Stuff it, Sal." Stepping out from behind the curtain, I take the mike from Victoria as Rosie sashays down the fifteen-foot runway, the lights at her feet flashing and throbbing with the rhythm of the music.

"It's your big day," I speak into the mike. The speakers squeal and I adjust the space between the mike and my mouth. The crowd's attention turns to me. "For many of us, it's all about family, right?"

No one reacts, not even Mama or Queenie in the audience. Both of them are frowning, confused at the sight of Tabby.

Undaunted, I continue. "Our pets are part of our family too, aren't they? We love them just like our kids. Why shouldn't they be included?"

A few nod. There's a smattering of murmurs. I'm not sure if I'm getting my point across or falling flat on my face.

"It's your day, and what will make it more special than including your pet in the ceremony, along with wearing an

Enchanted gown? Traditional weddings and beautiful ball-gowns fulfill our fantasies, but being yourself? That's price-less. If your dog, cat, or other pet is part of your family, they should be included as well."

More approving nods. I see people watching Rosie now, who's working it as she turns at the end of the stage, showing off the dress from all sides. Tabby cooperates and meows at the audience.

Light laughter breaks out over the tempo of the music, and everyone smiles or leans over to say something to the person next to them. As Rosie struts back past me, she winks.

She disappears behind the curtain, and Penn takes her place, striking a pose in the Ariel. As I talk about the design and drop more hints about being yourself, many of the younger gals make notes on their fliers.

Penn's tattoos and piercings pick up the overhead lights. When I mention finding a dress that accentuates your uniqueness, she makes sure to do a Vanna White impression, putting her inked forearms on full display as she strikes another pose at the end of the walkway.

To my surprise, and that of the crowd, Tabby strolls out, her marmalade body strutting like a model.

Rosie has placed a bling-y collar around her neck, which I recognize as one of our larger stretchy bracelets. People laugh and clap as Penn stops to scratch under her chin and Tabby raises her nose. The cat glances over the crowd acting like a majestic queen surveying her realm.

As Penn passes me, she winks like Rosie did and has a big smile on her face. I'm relieved, and I mention that we carry a full line of pet wedding accessories as well as bridal ones.

That's stretching it, but I know when to capitalize on an opportunity. First thing tomorrow, I'll have Rosie order a bunch.

As Tabby decides she rather enjoys being in the spotlight, Jenn appears. She's wearing my Snow White gown, which I named Winter. It has puffy half-sleeves, and while I didn't want to put color on it, the stripes of the classic dress worn by my inspiration are outlined by different materials in the bodice. The elegant train falls gracefully away from Jenn's slender frame, and in the back of my mind, I think about creating her dress.

The hint of an idea comes and goes as I talk about living your fairytale. Once again, I focus on the idea that every woman should have an unforgettable wedding that is unique to them.

Like Tabby, Jenn enjoys the attention, and she sits at the end, hugging Tabby and swinging her bare feet. This brings more applause. A few people snap photos.

I hope we're conveying that we are distinctive and special, and not simply amateurs as Sal has been claiming.

Out in the crowd, Tallulah materializes. She scowls at the people, the runway, and especially me. *If looks could kill*, I think.

I hope she waits to take out her anger until after the show.

She vanishes, and I draw a breath of relief. I scan the ballroom, but don't see her reappear. Glancing again to the lineup behind the curtain, I see Rosie. I allow Jenn and Tabby to have another moment before I mention all my designs are available to order at the fair and online.

Jenn gets the hint and finishes her stroll to return, Tabby following on her heels. As they go by, I give the audience members the website link.

Rosie glides out in the Bellamy, then Penn follows in the fifth, the unnamed. Gloria has made sure to sew and tuck all the seams into perfect placement, and I love the details she's added to this design.

As I watch Penn wear my favorite dress down the runway, I again imagine myself walking down the aisle with Logan on our wedding day.

It's then that I feel his eyes on me from the audience. He smiles when I catch his, and my world brightens. I love my life, even more so because of him.

After we're done, and Darinda and Sal are waiting to send their first model out, I realize that one of the women I saw with Sal isn't real. She's a ghost.

She isn't helping so much as simply hanging around. The lady I saw with him earlier when we arrived—Christine—is also flitting about, but the spirit helper is staring at me. As I remove a tiara from Penn's hair, and hold her gaze, she vanishes.

Older than Tallulah. Could it be her mother?

What concerns me is how I didn't know she was a ghost. That stops my hand in mid-air, still holding the elaborate accessory. I glance at the others in this backstage area, making sure I know who is in corporeal form and who's not.

Gah. There are so many of them, she could be anybody from the previous decades.

I see a bride off to one side, who I believed to be a model waiting to go, but as though she feels my fixed look on her, she glances my way. As soon as we connect, her image goes fuzzy and she fades to nothing.

I turn back toward the makeup table, a touch of dizziness coming over me.

"Are you okay?" Gloria reaches for my arm. "You look very pale, *cherie*."

Has my ghost radar gone wonky? "It's been a big day. I'm just tired."

Persephone appears behind her. "You need to find Tallulah. Now."

Meaning, I assume, the ghost is about to do something to

ruin the party. "Why don't you all go catch the rest of the show? I'm going to run to the restroom and splash water on my face."

Rosie offers to accompany me, but I tell her I'm fine. I just need a moment to breathe. Leaving behind the thumping music, I follow Persephone through a maze of hallways and up several flight of stairs. Sherlock—a ghost I picked up back at Christmas and thought had moved on—joins us.

"You're back," I say quietly.

He grins. "The game's afoot! Seph said you might need my genius expertise."

"I said no such thing," she denies.

Half of the light switches don't work, and I shun the dark hallways. A storm is brewing in the distance, lightning flashing here and there.

Following the two spirits, I find myself on the third floor, my guardian angel bopping in and out of several rooms. "Can't you find her?"

She sniffs. "She *was* here."

Most of the doors to the rooms are unlocked, and I do a visual scan of a few, but I *am* tired, the adrenaline of the day wearing off and leaving me drained. The fact there are so many ghosts in this hotel doesn't help. They keep flashing unexpectedly in front of me and winking out like old lights. They chill me to the bone and I feel more drained every time one passes by.

"Are the guests safe tonight?" I ask.

Sherlock looks skeptical. "Most likely."

Persephone and I come to a set of rooms that are locked. "These were the family's personal residences. A good place to search."

I make a shooing motion. "Well, go in and see."

She disappears through the wall, then reappears so quickly it startles me and I jump back, knocking into an antique table. The large vase on it tumbles to the side and I barely catch it before it hits the floor. "Nope. She's not in there, either," Persephone says.

I check my watch and notice it's almost time for the show to be over. "I've got to get back. Tallulah will have to wait."

As I head downstairs, trying not to freak out with all the dark shadows and the constant ghostly figures coming and going, I rub my arms and the goose flesh there.

Persephone and Sherlock bicker down the two flights, and I hear Baldwin wrapping things up once we reach the first floor. As I enter the area behind the stage, Darinda is looking around. "Have you seen Sal? He was here a minute ago."

"No, but when I do see him I have a few words for him. He's got a chip on his shoulder when it comes to me, and I don't know why. If I find out he had anything to do with damaging my dress or stealing my shoes—"

A woman screams, cutting me off.

I dart past my former boss and run in the direction of a set of decorative screens shoved in the shadowy corner. Sal's young assistant, in her street clothes once more, has a hand over her mouth as she stares at a spot behind one.

When I reach her, I suck in a breath at the sight. Sal, in his expensive suit and bow tie, is lying on the ground, unseeing eyes staring up. The tie is askew and a white bridal shoe sticks out of his throat, the heel soaked in blood

"Oh dear," I say.

Darinda rushes up behind me as blood pools on the floor. "What is it?"

"I've found Sal," I tell her.

And at least one of my missing shoes.

## ꩜ 4 ꩜

A thunderstorm rages outside as Detective Jones interrogates everyone.

He's mostly concerned with those who had access to the backstage during the runway show, but he still takes down all of the attendees' names and makes sure he has contact information for follow-up.

He leaves me until last. I'm totally exhausted and running on fumes. Logan rubs my back in support, as Mama, Queenie, Gloria, Rosie, Penn, and Jenn all gather around me like a shield.

Normally, I might think it silly. I can certainly take care of myself. But at the moment, having their strength and protection feels good.

As Jones, with his slow Southern drawl and flat eyes, goes through his set of questions, what little patience I have drains away. "Several others mentioned you had an antagonistic attitude toward the deceased." He holds a notepad but keeps his gaze pinned on me. "Would you care to fill me in on what that was all about?"

I'm slightly surprised, considering I thought I did a good

job hiding my true feelings about Sal. "He was the one who was antagonistic toward me. He kept criticizing my dresses and calling me amateurish."

"And that made you angry?"

I see where this is going. "I'm too tired to play games. I didn't kill the man. Happy?"

He takes his pen and points to the body, covered with a hotel room sheet. Blood stains the ivory material, and I swallow and look away. "That is your shoe in his throat, correct?"

"All of them went missing before the show started. I don't know where they are, and I don't know why someone would take them unless this was pre-meditated."

Jones lifts a bushy brow and makes a note. "I assume I'll find your prints on the murder weapon then?"

A string of curses fills my exhausted brain, but Mama squeezes my arm and I force myself to stay polite. She and Queenie stand over my shoulder, self-righteous indignation pouring off them. "I'm sure you will."

Another note and a long pause, his dark eyes searching my face, as if he can find my confession written on my forehead. "Now, where were you when this happened?"

I can't exactly tell him I was chasing a ghost, but for a minute, I consider doing so. A crack of thunder booms overhead, and we all flinch. Tabby makes a screeching noise and dives under the makeup table nearby. "I was chasing my cat," I tell him, thankful for the sudden inspiration.

It's clear he doesn't believe me in the way he tilts the corner of his lips down and writes on his pad.

"My daughter wouldn't hurt a fly," Mama says. She tugs on her blazer's hem, bristling with anger. Some of that is hiding fear, but I'm thankful for her adamant declaration.

Jones does not. "I'd appreciate it if y'all would stay out of my interrogation."

He gives Logan a stern glance, and Logan acts slightly aghast. "I thought this was simply a friendly questioning," he says to Jones. "Ava's not under suspicion, now is she?"

The detective and my boyfriend stare at each other in a showdown for a long minute. Jones puffs out his chest. "This would be a lot easier if I could speak to her alone."

Fat chance that. Logan's hand grips mine. "So you can harass my client more?"

Jones narrows his eyes. "Are you in need of an attorney, Miss Fantome?"

This man worked with my father on the Thornhollow department for many years, and he knows my family well. We've done this dance before, a couple times recently, when he believed my mother had a hand in the death of my aunt, and again when one of my father's former friends turned up dead in my front yard.

I have no love for the detective, and his attitude makes me come up off my seat. "While you're standing here trying to pin the murder on me, the killer is running around." I flap a hand in the general direction of the ballroom. "I know you have issues with me, but I had no reason to kill Sal, and I wouldn't hurt a fly, as Mama said."

Not exactly true—I don't like flies.

"If that's all, Detective Jones." Logan projects total confidence that it is. "We'll be going now."

Baldwin and Victoria are hovering across the way, trying to give us privacy while also not getting too close to the murder scene. Baldwin pipes up. "Detective Jones, can I get you a coffee?"

Jones slowly pivots and engages the hotel manager. "My team will be here to investigate the scene within the hour. You'll have to shut down this event."

Victoria nearly faints on the spot. "We can't do that, officer. I mean, no disrespect to the man who passed, but we have two hundred or more brides-to-be who've been waiting all year for this."

Baldwin has also paled considerably. A young woman with short blonde hair and big earrings emerges near his side and threads her fingers through his. This must be his wife. "The hotel's a big place," she says. "Surely, we can move the vendors into another wing and leave this area roped off for your investigators to work."

"Please," Victoria begs, bringing her hands in a prayer gesture to her chest. It's the first time I've seen her without her clipboard and overbearing attitude.

Jones taps his pen against his leg and screws up his lips again.

Mama, in all her affronted umbrage, is still mayor and knows many of her constituents in town are counting on this event bringing in the dollars. She steps around me and lowers her voice. "Landon, can't we work something out? Like Kalina said, this building is huge, there's plenty of space to move the event and the guests to. Besides, makes sense to keep everyone here, doesn't it? I don't know much about catching killers, but what if he or she is still here?"

Jones knows he's being played on some level, but he's a smart man. He realizes Mama is correct. With a big sigh, he puts his notepad in a jacket pocket and looks over those of us crowded into the backstage area. "No one is to come through here tonight once y'all leave. I'll post an officer to watch this area, but I want your word that all those vendor booths will be relocated, and no one will have access to this location until I give the okay."

I'm a little shocked he'd agree to their proposal, but on the other hand, I saw the way he slyly kept sending glances toward Victoria. He's been divorced for at least five years or more. Maybe his bachelorhood is starting to get old.

A glance at her left hand gives me hope. Maybe she's not

married either, and the good detective may find himself a little distracted during the next few days.

The lights flicker, and everyone holds their breath for a moment. We can't see the storm from here, but we can certainly hear the rain pelting down and the wind gusting.

My bones feel frosty again, and my weariness is suffocating. I wonder if Tallulah could've committed the murder. Persephone has been AWOL, as is her annoying habit, so I can't ask if she knows. I can't even find Sherlock now, who is usually more than willing to tag along and try to help.

It wouldn't be the first time I've encountered a spirit who conjured enough energy to manipulate objects, lights, and even plumbing. But to shove a shoe heel into someone's throat?

My attention drifts to the sheeted body. Why Sal?

If our killer *is* Tallulah, perhaps it was simply random, and he was convenient, but if it wasn't...?

Two men and one woman hustle in, long raincoats and hats dripping water. Kalina dashes out, saying she'll get towels, and they speak to Jones and apologize for taking so long to arrive.

"The weather out there is nasty," a tall, thin man tells him. "The road from town is flooded. We had to drive a few miles out of the way to get here."

Jones instructs us to move from behind the curtain and onto the stage so the team can get to work. I overhear Baldwin talking anxiously to Victoria about the bad publicity. We stand in a group, waiting for Jones to join us and give us the official word we're dismissed.

I'm about to leave regardless. I see the ghosts from earlier reenacting their loops again in the giant ballroom. My head hurts and my feet ache from being on them all day. All I want is to get home and go to bed.

"That doesn't sound good about the roads," Queenie says. Mama nods in agreement.

"I'm so tired I could fall off the stage and not even care," Rosie adds.

Penn and Jenn sit below in the audience area, still crammed with chairs. Penn calls up to me, "Can we leave now?"

Jones struts out, his stride as slow as his drawl. "*May* we," he corrects her. "You can try, but it sounds like you'll have a long drive to town. You'll have to take the county road north of here since the main one is washed out."

"Oh dear." Gloria wrings her hands. "I think I'll stay here tonight. I don't like driving in the dark, especially during a storm."

Logan nods. "That's a good idea." He checks his watch. "It's after midnight. Who knows how long this will go on? And the county road isn't a whole lot better than the main one."

Jenn jumps up. "A sleepover! We can make popcorn and watch an old movie."

Penn stands as well and stretches. "That sounds like fun."

Baldwin hails us. "We're happy to put your group on the third floor in connecting suites. They're normally unused, but Kalina and I will give you a discount, and we'll send up food."

How generous. Queenie says to Kalina, "I can prepare meals for everyone if you show me the way to the kitchen."

"That would be appreciated," she responds.

"If you give me clean sheets," Mama offers, "I'll fix up the beds."

Kalina motions for them to follow her and Baldwin claps his hands. "You'll need flashlights—this storm will play havoc with the electricity. The Wi-Fi is free, btw."

I'm more concerned about the lights than using the internet, but I thank him. He and his wife seem genuinely happy to have more guests.

"I'll close up the booth," Rosie tells me.

Penn and Jenn help her down. "We'll get the dresses in the garment bags," Penn volunteers.

I sink to the edge of the stage and am slightly surprised when Tabby rushes from the runway to stand in my lap. She rubs her head on my chest, and I scratch behind her ears. "I suppose you're hungry."

No surprise, she meows loudly in reply.

Baldwin returns with flashlights and keys to the suites. Logan takes my hand and pulls me to my feet. He leads me from the ballroom, past the expansive lobby, and to an elevator I wish I'd noticed earlier. He talks about Jones and the murder, but my ears are ringing, my limbs weak, and I can barely force any reply.

I've never had such a drastic reaction to ghostly energy, but I've also never been surrounded by so many.

On the third floor, we exit, and Logan flips on lights which flicker as though threatening to go out. Down the vast corridor, we pass multiple rooms. I was here earlier.

There's a large, arched window at the end, a portrait of the family across from a set of massive wooden double doors. As Logan slides the antique key into the lock, lightning flashes outside.

On its heels, thunder rocks the hotel, the window pane rattles and the lights go out.

Save a few flickering phantoms, we're plunged into darkness.

There's literally nothing better than spending a night in a haunted hotel, I tell myself, which is a total lie.

A hard shove sends me sprawling into Logan. He drops the key, the metal clanking on the wooden floor. The flashlight sails out of my hand, careening into the corner.

Logan rights me, and I grab the flashlight once more. He retrieves the key, and I shine the beam around, seeing no one there but Tabby. The cat is watching the portrait on the wall across from us. The Nottingham family stares back.

"Did you do that?" I snap at her, but she ignores me, remaining focused.

Emanuele Nottingham sits in a brocade chair, one leg crossed over the other, a pipe in hand. Mary Mae stands slightly behind him, a hand on the winged back.

In front of her, and on Emanuele's left stands a solemn young girl, probably ten or eleven. At their feet, sits a beautifully groomed black and white spaniel.

The perfect family.

Logan unlocks the door. "Let me guess. There are ghosts?"

At least I don't have to keep my 'gift' a secret from him.

Before I can confirm that there are, indeed, many still enjoying the hotel, a whisper of one glides through the wall near the portrait and disappears.

Tabby turns and blinks at me.

"The place is haunted," I confirm. "But, like, on steroids. It's creeping me out."

Footsteps echo from the other end, and a light at the steps dances over the wall as Mama arrives panting. "Oh, there you are. The elevator went out with the electricity, and there are so many stairs." Her arms are filled with linens and blankets. Logan rushes to help her.

Inside the main suite, it's a museum. The living area greets us, with a large fireplace, built-in bookshelves, and an over-abundance of furniture straight out of the twenties. There are more family portraits, and I see the strong resemblance between the ghost of Tallulah and her mother.

There's a wheelchair in one corner, cobwebs dripping from its frame. The various tables, as well as the mantle, have a thick coat of dust.

As we meander through the other rooms, scads of dust particles reflect in the illumination from the flashlight. A main bedroom contains separate twin beds. Prudish, but I assume this room belonged to Tallulah's parents. A giant armoire and neat rows of shoes suggest she never got rid of her parent's belongings.

Yep, creepy.

In the kitchen, we find several modern-day appliances. A microwave, a decent refrigerator, and a matching stove reveal that Tallulah at least updated a few things in her later years. The old wallpaper and cabinets stand in stark contrast.

A second smaller bedroom holds a young girl's mementos and more heavy furniture. Mama begins stripping the bed of its quilted comforter and sneezes. "It's so dusty. I feel like I've gone back in time."

My heavy limbs slow me as I help her put fresh sheets on. Once we complete that task, we discover Logan in the living room, checking the flue. "I'd try to get a fire going," he says, brushing his hands together, "but this hasn't been used in years. I'm afraid it might set the whole place a blaze."

I'm slightly disappointed. I hadn't thought about a fire, but one might warm me up, and the idea of it seems comforting.

There are oil lamps, and he does manage to find matches and light those, so we have an easier time moving about. Mama points at a stack of linens she placed on the couch and sets her gaze on him. "I assume you're taking that tonight?"

Logan and I exchange a glance, and he nods. "Of course, Mrs. Fantome." Always the gentleman.

Rosie, Penn, and Jenn arrive, Rosie looking like death warmed over, while the sisters seem totally jazzed about sleeping here. I direct Rosie into the master, and Mama offers to help her sheet one of the beds. Penn and Jenn will take a room farther down the hall and leave the connecting one for Mama, Queenie, and Gloria.

Queenie shows up and motions us to help her find the dumbwaiter she says must be in the kitchen. Sure enough, we discover a door to the hidden elevator, and Logan hauls up the food Queenie loaded onto it.

Gathering around one of the oil lamps at the kitchen table Penn has scrubbed clean, we dig into sandwiches and soup. All but Rosie, who screws up her face and dashes for the bathroom at the scent of food. Tabby is happy to eat the turkey slice from her sandwich.

Gloria's cell rings and she leaves to take the call.

"I remember my mother talking about this place when I was a kid," Mama says.

Queenie nods. "This old hotel is full of history. Some of it not so good."

The two older women recite a few bits and pieces of stories they've heard. Mama mentions that one of her uncles stayed here after he came home from World War II.

"Why?" I ask.

"Shell shock." She finishes off her soup and pushes the bowl away. "They call it PTSD now, but this place was used for soldiers suffering from that and other ailments for a time. They promised the fresh air and quiet would restore their good health."

"A psych ward?" Penn looks intrigued.

"No, not like that." Queenie refills her glass at the sink. "They were here of their own free will and received a minimum of medical care. It was more to recuperate, and Lord knows, they needed it. Poor men."

When we're done, we're all too tired to do the dishes, and simply load them in the sink. Mama tells us she'll wash them in the morning.

As everyone adjourns to their various rooms, Logan gives me a parting kiss. "Have you seen Salvatore's ghost?" he whispers. "He could tell you who killed him."

That's the one I *haven't* seen. I shrug. "No dice yet. He didn't much like me in life, he probably doesn't even realize I'm a medium in death. Even if he did, knowing him, he's still a diva. Right now, I don't care if he *does* appear. I'm going to bed."

In Tallulah's bedroom, I put the flashlight on the nightstand and look around. There's another armoire here. More shoes lined up next to it.

Definitely a Type A personality.

An open book rests on a small table near the window, a chair next to it. Under the binding is part of a puzzle that was never finished. The nightstand holds a lamp, a pair of spectacles, and a bottle of perfume.

Curiosity gets the best of me, and I check the drawer.

Inside I find a picture frame. I pull it out and see a sepia-toned photo of a man in uniform.

Was this Tallulah's boyfriend? Persephone said she never married, but maybe she was still sweet on one of the guys who returned from the war.

As I crawl under the covers, I think about Sal again. Death by stiletto seems like an odd way to go, but also ironically fitting. He was totally immersed in bridal wear and the business.

Christine pops into my head. He was so hard on her, and she definitely had the means to surprise him with an attack. She also had opportunity.

She "discovered" the body.

I send out an SOS to Persephone, but she doesn't appear, and I decide it's up to me to investigate the woman further.

*Tomorrow*, I promise myself as I drift off to sleep.

## ❦ 6 ❧

The next morning, the storm has passed. Baldwin has the electricity working, and, after a quick breakfast, we begin moving the vendors to a smaller ballroom near the atrium and courtyard.

Wandering the halls, I'm once again amazed at the architecture and details. It's truly a historic establishment, if a bit run down. The number of ghosts that still linger is also amazing, and not in a good way.

I send Logan to Thornhollow to pick up clean clothes and a few essentials for me. Queenie leaves as well, heading for her restaurant to get what she's prepared for tonight's tasting event. Caterers and bakeries will be offering samples of reception items and wedding cakes, and as Queenie likes to say, "Food always brings folks in."

Logan texts to let me know the main road is still barricaded, and the route around it will take longer than expected.

Rosie is gleeful, although still wan. She's nearly as pale as the ghosts. Overnight, we've received three dress orders and two brides want to schedule consults. It's good to see her perkier, and she's quite proud of the fact she hasn't tossed her meager breakfast of toast and tea.

By mid-morning, Logan reports in to tell us the main road to town has a huge tree down, thanks to the storm, and that's why it's closed. The county road commissioner has sent a crew to clear it, but attendance that day at the fair may be lower than expected, since it will be more challenging for people to get here from the south.

Mama jumps to attention at this news and hustles off to call the commissioner.

Several dozen brides with their mothers and bridesmaids stayed the night, and as we resume our booth, they filter in. Folks from other areas begin arriving as well.

Some are curiosity seekers, who've heard about Sal's murder. Others already purchased tickets for the day, and if it's one thing I know about brides, they're undaunted.

The afternoon is a whirl of women of all ages looking for dresses, accessories, party planning, and more. Victoria comes to tell us the tasting is sold out.

Photographers, trip advisors, gift suppliers, and even an ordained minister not affiliated with a church offer their products and services. While this space is still big enough to fit half a football field in it, the booths are crammed together.

Detective Jones stops in and pulls me aside. After several minutes of another interrogation, I'm fed up with his attitude. Logan arrives in time to rescue me and brings a late lunch, along with fresh clothes and makeup bags Queenie has supplied.

Knowing the fair would be filled with long days, I asked Brax and Rhys, my next-door neighbors, to take care of my cats, Arthur and Lancelot. Throughout the afternoon, Tabby makes appearances, but I don't worry too much about her. She receives more than enough attention from the visitors, and seems to keep an eye on Christine and Darinda.

Logan and I find a private spot in the atrium to chat and share a sandwich. While there are a few meandering among the roses and greenery, it's fairly quiet.

"Jones doesn't have anyone else who looks good for the murder," Logan tells me. "You're one of the few people who doesn't have an alibi for the time of the death."

I swallow a mouthful of Queenie's chicken salad and sip iced tea. "We can't be sure Sal was murdered. Maybe he realized my gowns would be a huge success and couldn't stand it. He picked up a stiletto and plunged it into his own throat."

Logan offers a forced smile at my attempt at poor humor. "Good to see you have your sarcastic wit today. I was kind of worried about you last night."

"I thought long and hard on what happened. I have a suspect."

"Who?"

"Sal's assistant, Christine. She had means, motive, and opportunity. I'm not sure what her alibi is during that stretch of ten minutes when Sal was killed, but I plan to keep an eye on her."

"Well, watch your back. I'll see if I can get anything out of Jones about her, and I'll look into her background." He wads up his paper napkin and crumples the bag the food came in. "I have an afternoon appointment, but I can cancel if you want me to stay."

"I'll be fine." I finish off my sandwich. "Keep it and see what you can get out of Jones. We'll connect again later, okay?"

After kissing me, he leaves, and I return to the booth. There's another of Queenie's white paper bags, and inside are heart-shaped sugar cookies with thick frosting. Of course, every time I start to take a bite, another bride steps up to the table, surrounded by her mother and bridesmaids.

Mama is busy gossiping with a group of local gals and Penn and Jenn have yet to make an appearance.

Eventually, Rosie and I decide we'll have to take shifts. She can't eat much anyway and ends up flying solo while I down my cookie. Gloria is flushed when she returns from a walk to the horse stables and back, and talks nonstop about the sweeping staircases, decorative finials, and moldings.

"I have so many ideas!" She pulls out a sketchbook. With that and one of the treats in hand, she disappears once more, claiming she's off to the hotel's immense library.

I text Brax to thank him again for taking care of my cats, and he replies to tell me he plans to attend the tasting.

Darinda rushes past, and after making sure Rosie's okay with the number in line to talk to us, I sneak off to grab her.

Christine is behind the Southern Bride table, looking harried from all of the potential clients lining up there as well. When Darinda sees me, I ask if I can speak to her in private. While Christine frowns, she breaks away and motions me toward the rear of the tent.

Christine stands to show a bride a display of headpieces, and sends me a glare. Darinda and I slip through the tent flaps.

I lower my voice and gesture to Christine. "How well do you know her?"

Darinda frowns. "Why?"

"I heard Sal putting her down a lot yesterday. Did they get along?"

Darinda laughs self-consciously. "You can't be serious. Are you insinuating what I think you are?"

"She doesn't seem too upset about him being dead."

My former boss puts a hand on her hip in a gesture I'm well acquainted with. "Ava, what has gotten into you?"

Her tone reminds me of Mama's when I'm annoying her

with too many questions. "We could have a murderer in our midst, and I don't feel comfortable about that."

Her gaze slides to Christine, who we can see through the flap.

Now, she lowers her voice, too, and I can barely hear her over the noise. "Sal was a bit of a prima donna. You know that. But he knew how to close sales, and he was good at his job. Maybe not quite as good as you, but I wouldn't say he had enemies, and certainly not Christine."

Before I can respond, I swear I hear Sal's voice. "What's going on here?"

I pivot, scanning the area but don't see anything except the living and the backside of the tents. I start to call his name then think better of it. Darinda doesn't know I can see and speak to ghosts. I'd rather keep it that way.

"Detective Jones believes I'm the most likely suspect at the moment, and I'd like to rid him of that idea if possible. I'm not trying to place blame on an innocent woman, but again, we all need to be careful because the culprit is still on the loose."

She gives me a long, thoughtful look and slips back inside.

I walk slowly along the rear of the booths. "Sal?" I stage whisper. "Can you hear me? Are you here?"

The din of the crowd covers up my voice, but I know spirits can hear me, no matter how softly I speak.

"I don't understand..."

It's him again. I can't see him, but he must be nearby. Occasionally this happens when ghosts can't materialize, and there's still enough energy coming through that I can hear their voice. "You're dead," I say quietly. "You need to tell me who killed you."

"*Dead?*"

It's a screech, half-shocked and half-you're-pulling-my-leg.

"I know that must be upsetting, but please try hard to

think about what happened. Who was the last person you remember seeing?"

I feel a breeze flutter around my face, and then it disappears. So does his voice. I stand there waiting, my chest tight, but he doesn't answer.

I try to sense if he's still here, but it's just empty air, the sounds of the brides and the vendors echoing off the high ceilings and the wallpaper.

Deflated, I put out another SOS to Persephone.

Crickets, in response.

I move to the front of the tents, scanning the area. Apparitions of men with haunted expressions fade in and out. Nurses in white uniforms do as well.

Returning to the Enchanted booth, I see Rosie unpacking another mannequin from a storage box while there's a break in the rush. "Help me get this together so we can put the Ariel on it. Potential clients want to see the gowns, touch them. I think it'll be a big day for us."

"I'll do it. You grab the dress."

She retrieves the garment bag and unzips it, as I screw the head on. Penn and Jenn stroll in and tell us they've been sitting in the courtyard, discussing ideas for Jenn's wedding in June.

"Ava, look at this."

Rosie lifts the skirt, and in the dim light, I squint as I examine the hem. "It looks like it's been dragged through the mud."

I reach out and touch the satin, disbelief making me question what I'm seeing. Sure enough, fine particles crumble under my fingers, leaving behind dirty stains. "How did this happen? It was just worn in the show last night and it was fine."

"Jenn wore it," she confirms, and the younger sister nods.

"I took it off afterward, and we hung it up. I swear it was okay then."

We glance at each other, baffled. I pull it into a better light. "The material doesn't look as if it was ever wet. How did it end up with mud on it?"

Penn moves closer and runs her fingers along the soiled hem. "It's just like the other one with the stain on the bodice. Who's doing this?"

I suspected Sal of that. Was it possible he committed this act, too, before he was killed?

And if not him, who? One of the vendors? Would anyone stoop so low to sabotage me?

I shake my head, wondering about the timeline, and how Sal or anyone else could have accomplished this. "Has anyone seen the missing shoes?"

The others shake their heads.

I'm dumbfounded. "Maybe if we could find those, I could discover a clue pointing to whoever did this. Meanwhile, I'll see if I can wash the worst of this off."

Penn and Jenn offer to stay with Rosie. I take the gown inside the garment bag to the nearest restroom, along with stain remover Rosie was smart enough to pack. There was no time to use it last night, but I put a generous amount along the hem of this one and let it soak.

Even the restrooms here are stunning. There's a sitting area with a wall of mirrors and a makeup table, a separate lavatory with stalls.

Lost in thought, I startle when Tallulah appears in front of me. "You don't belong here! Leave my stuff alone!"

I check to make sure I'm truly alone. Seems the coast is clear. "Tallulah, dear, you're the one who doesn't belong here. You died in 2004, and you need to cross over and stay there."

She makes a face and glides away, mumbling. Then she jets

back. "This place is mine. I don't want all these people here, and especially not you!"

I'm affronted. "Why not me?"

She vanishes. Sometimes I think it must be nice to be a ghost—you can simply disappear if you want to have the final say in a conversation.

"Did you kill Sal?" I call after her.

There's no answer, and she doesn't return. Eventually, I wash off the hem. The stain remover has done a pretty good job, and I doubt anyone will notice.

I run it under the blow dryer and return to the booth. Penn assists me in clothing the mannequin and we relieve Rosie with the next group who come by to see the catalog and talk about an upcoming Roaring Twenties-themed wedding.

"The Bellamy is what I want," the petite brunette bride states to her mother.

"But I've always dreamed of you in a ballgown like the Ella," her mother replies.

This is a conundrum Rosie and I seem to encounter often. "The best thing to do," I suggest, "is to come to The Wedding Chapel and try on both. See which you fall in love with."

While I make an appointment for the bride to do that, Gloria returns and sinks into a chair nearby. Her sketchpad is open and she mocks up a series of gowns over the next few minutes that have me feeling a bit motivated to draw myself. As I continue to make appointments and show off my designs, Gloria and I brainstorm new ideas.

Eventually, I decide to take a break and go upstairs to the suite. I freshen my makeup, brush my teeth, and make a pot of coffee. Filling a travel mug I find in a cabinet, I take it with me downstairs.

I meet Kalina coming from the outdoor courtyard when I near the ballroom.

She eyes the mug. "You know, the kitchen is down that hallway on the left. There's almost always some brewing. You don't have to go upstairs for a cup."

"Oh, thank you. That would be a lot handier."

She smiles and leans in as if sharing a secret. "If you need something a touch stronger later, the bar is off the lobby, past the check-in desk. We don't have a full-time bartender, but I can pour you a stiff one if you need it."

"I appreciate the offer." I raise my cup in salute. A nightcap isn't the worst idea. "I may take you up on that."

There's an hour left before the tasting event, and I'm hungry. Rosie won't get much out of the food samples, and she's been on her feet all day. I hand her her coat and tell her to go home and see her husband and son.

"You sure?"

"Of course. I'll get the scoop on the out-of-town caterers and bakeries and do some networking so we can build relationships with them."

I walk her to the rear of the building and out to the parking lot, leaving Penn and Jenn to close up the booth. The air warmed after the storm, but as the sun sets, I feel the temperature dropping. As she drives off, I sip my coffee and breathe in the cool, February air. It feels nice to take a break from the constant ruckus of the fair, and smell something other than the past. No dust, and the simple act of being in such a beautiful spot relaxes the tension in my shoulders.

Taking a stroll past the atrium, I notice a small cemetery in the distance. The stones barely peek out from all the overgrowth. They seem to be centered around an old oak tree, the Spanish moss hanging from the giant branches still weighed down from last night's rain.

Tabby rubs against my leg, startling me, and I nearly spill

my drink. I scold her and she saunters off toward the tree. I see Persephone sitting on a low-hanging branch, swinging her legs and beckoning me. Sherlock leans on the massive trunk, saying something I can't hear but that makes her smile.

With a sigh, I follow the cat to see who's buried in the sad, little graveyard.

## 7

The markers are nearly hidden under years of dirt, weeds, and melancholy.

I scrape mud from last night's storm from one of the concrete forms, pitted and moss-stained. Emanuele Nottingham, it reads. Tallulah's father. A smaller stone next to it is a little fresher—her mother.

Debris tangles around my ankles as I move to the most modern looking, another plain and simple design. Tallulah Nottingham is etched in with a single lily flower, the slender neck bent so it appears as if it's tired.

"Why did you call me over?" I ask Persephone.

Exasperation laces her tone. "I have to feed you everything on a silver platter."

Sherlock chastises her before I can reply. "Seph, be kind."

She rolls her eyes and slides off the branch. "She has work to do and she's off playing happily-ever-after."

"*She* is standing right here, and as you say, I do have work to do." I rub my arms through my light clothing. "What is it you want?"

I don't see or sense any spirits lingering here, but the

place would be perfect for a ghost story or a reality show featuring paranormal investigators.

Sherlock hovers and Persephone grumbles. "Have a peek around."

Picking my way in the direction Sherlock pointedly looks, I note a side of the once-white wooden fence is sagging. The paint has faded under the Georgia sun and years of weather. Nearby magnolia bushes haven't been trimmed in some time.

A dingy stone under a younger oak, and nearly hidden by the magnolias, catches my eye. The rectangular marker barely sticks up above the ground, the earth around it seeming to suck it in. Using my hand, I pull a cluster of overgrown weeds from it and trace a finger along the single word inscribed there: Monroe.

There are no birth or death dates. I rise when I hear footsteps behind me, noticing Persephone and Sherlock have disappeared.

I turn to find Christine marching toward me, fire in her eyes. "Darinda told me what you said. I can't believe you think I killed Sal."

*Thanks a lot*, I mentally say to my former boss. "It wasn't my intent to accuse anyone; I was simply asking a few questions about your relationship with him. He was pretty hard on you, wasn't he?"

She's wearing high heels and doesn't want to stomp through the mud and weeds, so she stops a few yards away at a section of the fencing that's still intact. "So what? I've never had a job yet where a superior treats you like an equal. He may have given me a lot of grief, but I would never kill anyone."

She crosses her arms, and I notice how thin they are. I wonder if she would even have the strength to shove a heel into a man's throat. I don't know exactly how much pressure that'd take, but she looks as though lifting weights is not a regular habit, and seems to lack that killer instinct I would expect. Anger, like the kind I see in her face right now, however, might do the task.

"Whoever killed him got up close and personal." I overheard the medical examiner mention to Jones last night that there were no defensive wounds she could see on the first examination. "Can you think of anyone else who would want to do Sal harm?"

The young woman's eyes narrow. I'm probably only a few years older than she is, but I feel as though there's a vast difference in maturity. She taps a foot. "Nobody cared for that man. You of all people know that."

"Darinda claims he didn't have enemies. Do you agree?"

She rolls her eyes and uncrosses her arms in a dramatic wave. "You're starting to sound like that detective. I didn't know Sal personally, but no one at the bridal salon liked him. We had to tolerate him because he was Darinda's pet. She needed someone, I guess, to fill that spot you left."

I hear someone call my name from the parking lot, and see Gloria flagging me down. It's nearly time for the tasting event. I wave back.

"I saw you take that dress to the restroom. Why? Did it have blood on it?" Christine acts like she's caught me with my hand in the cookie jar.

"Blood?"

"Don't worry." She pivots to return to the hotel. "I already texted the detective to let him know I saw what you were doing. I bet they can do some forensic thing to see if it's Sal's blood."

Sighing, I take one last glance at the Monroe marker and go to meet Gloria.

"A few vendors are keeping their booths open, *ma cherie*. It's a good marketing strategy. Do you want me to man yours while you network? Penn and Jenn can help."

"You need to go home and get some rest. Tomorrow's Saturday, they should have the road cleared, and it's the biggest day yet. I need you to be ready to roll."

"Don't be silly. I'm fine."

Mama's exiting the back to leave. We catch up, and she asks if I'm going home.

I have a mystery to solve and a murderer to find. "I'm going to stay overnight again. I want to schmooze with the caterers and bakeries, and I'm inspired to work on a new design." I motion at the hotel, looking it over. "This place is full of nostalgia, and it gives me a lot of ideas for my flapper line."

I kiss Mama goodbye. As I return inside with Gloria, Tabby once again makes her presence known.

My friend is a sucker for her neediness and Gloria rubs her ears. "Since you're not keeping your stand active, I'm going to attend the taste testing with Penn and Jenn. I want to get some of that wine from the Cross vineyard." She winks. "I've heard it's pretty good."

Logan's family owns it, and they do make a good product. "Absolutely. You go ahead."

As she walks to the atrium with the sisters, Victoria glides by the open doors. She's talking a million miles a minute to someone walking with her.

Christine.

Between the ghosts and the killer, I wonder how smart it is for me to spend another night in this hotel.

## 8

I do a cursory swing through the vendors, grabbing a few samples here and there to fill my empty stomach. I avoid the wine Gloria is enjoying since I have some legwork to do and I need a clear head.

I can't dodge Logan's mother, however, and chat with her a moment or two at their table. There are multiple wines available for tasting and cases behind her with bottles to purchase.

"I heard there was a situation with you and another man last night," Helen says, handing a sample to Gloria of their famous peach wine.

Her hair is properly swept up and diamonds hang from her lobes. Her dress is gold, like the tablecloth, and she's wearing a berry-colored scarf that perfectly matches the red merlot available. She gives me a look that suggests she's annoyed I may once again be tainting her son's reputation.

"Oh, it wasn't her fault." Gloria takes a sip and licks her lips. "She didn't kill him."

A bride and her fiancé give a shocked gasp and move away.

Helen harrumphs and pours a few more samples, lowering her voice. "Why is it that trouble follows you everywhere, Ava?"

I honestly have no answer to that.

Gloria makes a dismissive noise. "What are you talking about? Ava is a good girl!"

"Thank you, Gloria." I glance around the atrium, noticing more tasters headed our direction. Victoria is also making rounds. No use arguing with Helen, and I have more pressing matters to attend to. A part of me wants to avoid Victoria as well. "Good luck with the sales," I say and beeline to a booth I actually want to visit.

Queenie has put Brax to work, the mother and son duo moving in perfect harmony as they handle potential clients for her catering service. When I get there, Brax comes around to envelope me in a bear hug, and nearly squeezes the small amount of food and drink I've enjoyed back out.

He beams from ear to ear as he sets me on my feet. He's looking sharp in a turquoise colored dress shirt and fancy tie. "This is fabulous, isn't it? I can't believe how many are here!"

He towers over me and his mother, but she pokes his side and motions for him to hand out more food to the those crowding in. She has a generous assortment of down-home, Southern items on her list, along with melt-in-your-mouth desserts and candy.

Brax is every bit as much an entrepreneur as his mother, and he's happy to dispense cards advertising his and his partner's various businesses: The Thorny Toad, their roadside bar and grill, his coffee bar downtown, as well as their lovely bed & breakfast next to The Wedding Chapel. Brax shoves several of Queenie's shrimp boil skewers at me, along with mini-mushroom and goat cheese pot pies.

"Honey, you look a fright." He drags me behind the table

and fiddles with my hair. "Those bags under your eyes could carry ten pound weights in them."

He's honest, if nothing else, which is one of the reasons I love him like a brother. "It's been a rough twenty-four hours."

He sneaks some sliced cucumbers from a cooler and lays them on my plate. "Go lie down and put these on your eyes for twenty minutes, y'hear?"

Upstairs in the suite, I finish my food, which is so good I contemplate returning for more. I eat the cucumber rather than waste the slices on my eye bags. I suspect those aren't going away anytime soon.

I remove the photo from the nightstand and stare at it. When I hear the cooing of a child again, I nearly drop the frame. There's no ghost to be seen, but like so many things here, this random spirit is beginning to wear on my nerves.

Opening my laptop, I plan to answer some email, but end up doing a search for the name Monroe in combination with the hotel. I get zip back.

I try several others, but without more information, I discover nothing. I snap a picture with my phone and do a reverse image search. Again, zero.

Downstairs, I discover Logan has arrived. He catches me as I exit the elevator, and kisses my cheek. "How's it going?"

"Busy. Are you here to help your mom?"

"I offered but she told me I had my work cut out for me corralling you and keeping you out of trouble. I take it you spoke to her?"

I head for the front desk. "She seems to have jumped to the conclusion I'm the cause of last night's fiasco."

He chuckles. "You know Thornhollow. Lot of rumors flying. Gossip, too. Your name was mentioned."

"Of course it was." Kalina is manning the desk and I show her the photo. "Could this guy be related to the Nottingham family?"

She gives me a glance suggesting she has better things to do. "How would I know?"

"This was in Tallulah's nightstand. Have you seen pictures of him anywhere else here?"

She studies it a moment, pursing her lips to the left. "There could be family photo albums in the study."

"Where's that?"

"Down the hall from the suites. Next to the elevator, but on the other side. It's full of old books, magazines, and newspapers. I swear that woman never got rid of anything."

"Tallulah?"

She nods.

"Why didn't *you?*" Logan asks.

She glances away and gives an involuntary shudder. "I started to once, but it was so overwhelming, and... Well, it's spooky in there."

I have the feeling by that she means haunted. "Then is it possible the hotel still has the logs from after the war when this was used as a sort of hospital?"

Kalina shrugs. "No idea, but probably. In that study alone there are all kinds of old records."

"Thank you."

Logan follows me to the elevator. "What's going on? Did I miss something important?"

"Just a usual day in the life of Ava Fantome." I smile at him and peck his cheek as we wait for the doors to slide open. "Full of ghosts and murderers."

He smiles, motioning for me to go first. "Never a dull moment with you, that's for sure."

The doors are about to shut when Gloria's ghost appears, and I nearly drop the framed picture again. "You must hurry. She's ill."

I grab the door to keep it from shutting. "Who? Gloria?"

"What...?" Logan follows my gaze. "Wait... A ghost?"

"Hurry!" The spirit fades away.

"Come with me," I say to Logan, jetting back into the lobby. "I think Gloria's in trouble."

We run to the atrium, pushing past people in the lobby, hallway, and outside the courtyard. They're talking and laughing, enjoying the samples, and the noise is loud. When we enter the glass enclosure, I hear someone yelling for help.

Gloria's prone on the floor near the mermaid water fountain, struggling and grabbing at her neck. I see Tallulah on top of her, ghostly hands wrapped around her throat.

*How is she doing that?*

Victoria is on her knees next to her, trying to help. "She's choking!"

I shove the photo into Logan's hands and grab the first metal thing I find—a garden trowel.

Gloria's male ghost is also here and he reaches for Tallulah. As he shoves at her, I slice the trowel through the air, right at Tallulah's heart. She screeches, raising the hair on my arms, and the metal creates a sparking effect as it cuts through her spectral form.

All at once, she freezes, her gaze coming up to meet mine. I see surprise in her eyes, along with anger, right before her body disintegrates.

Metal often works on spirits, although it won't keep her away for long.

Gloria coughs and chokes as Logan and I help her sit up.

Her ghost bends down next to her and Victoria displays an obvious shiver and backs away. "Is she all right?"

Helen, Brax, and a few others form a crowd around us. "She'll be okay now," I say. "We'll take it from here."

Tears run down Gloria's cheeks and Logan hands her a napkin from a nearby booth. Victoria chases off the gawkers, as we get Gloria to a chair. Brax disappears then arrives with a bottled water.

"Thank you," I tell him.

Between sips, Gloria swears she wasn't choking on a sample. "I don't know what...happened." Her voice is rough and raw. "One minute I was enjoying salmon on toast...the next this heavy weight knocked me to the floor. I...I...couldn't breathe."

Baldwin runs in and looks her over. "Does she need an ambulance?"

"No, no." Taking another drink, she shakes her head adamantly. "I'm fine. Really."

"A weight?" Logan questions.

Gloria is too pale. "Felt like a linebacker hit me."

He pats her shoulder and gives me a glance that asks ghost? I nod.

"You really should see Doc," I tell her. "Let him check you out. For my peace of mind, if nothing else. Remember, I need you in top form tomorrow."

She doesn't argue this time, and I'm relieved. Most everyone has returned to the wining and dining and Logan and I help Gloria to her feet since she's still wobbly.

"You definitely should," Brax says.

"I'll drive her to the clinic." Logan motions for Brax to take her arm and he hands the framed photo back to me. "I'll bring the car to the rear door."

Slowly, Brax and I assist her. Baldwin follows, wringing his hands. Logan pulls up in his Porsche and we guide Gloria into it.

"I'll call you as soon as I make sure she's okay," he tells me and then they're gone.

Victoria appears from a side hallway and walks with us as we make our way once more to the lobby. "Your friend is all right?"

"You don't think she'll say anything about this, do you?" Baldwin asks.

"I think so," I tell Victoria, but I'm confused by Baldwin's question and give him a questioning glance. "Say anything...?"

Victoria nods. "We don't need more bad publicity, and we especially don't need her telling people she choked on Lamar's prized hors d'oeuvres."

I don't know or care who Lamar is, and since I know Gloria didn't choke on the food, I just roll my eyes. "Gloria isn't one to stir up drama."

"We'll make it up to her." Baldwin assures me. "I'll send her a gift card or something."

"There are at least a dozen people who witnessed the incident," Brax reminds them. "I'm sure it's already on social media."

Victoria sighs loudly. "It wasn't the event's fault."

Her concern about that over a person's life irritates me, but I just want her and Baldwin to skedaddle. "No one is going to blame you. Look, a bite went down the wrong way, that's all, and Gloria won't cause any trouble."

Reassured, they hustle off to get everyone back into a festive mood. Brax pats my shoulder. "Was there something supernatural about what happened to Gloria?"

He also knows about and encourages my gift. "It's a long story. I'll tell you about it one of these days."

He nods and returns to his mother's table. I head to the elevator, and end up with Jenn and Penn grabbing my arms.

"I thought this tasting event would be more fun," Jenn says.

"Is Gloria okay?" Penn asks. "We were in the courtyard, but heard she choked on a sample."

"Logan's taking her to see Doc, but I think she'll be fine." *Especially if she's not here with Tallulah, the angry ghost.*

"Kalina gave us a deck of cards and two board games." Jenn grins from ear to ear. "We thought we'd have a girl party. Like a true sleepover."

Penn punches the button, and the doors open right up. The two of them haul me inside.

"We've got microwave popcorn, too," Penn adds, selecting the third floor and showing me a stack of the plastic wrapped bags.

Great, just what I need. They're determined to get their girly party, and it looks like I won't be alone tonight again.

I only hope the ghosts give me a break.

## ❧ 9 ❧

After a game of gin rummy, two of Clue, and one of Operation, the three of us fall asleep on the couch watching a vintage James Cagney movie.

I wake up with arms and legs entangled with mine, the smell of popcorn lingering in the air. Logan called during the second round of Clue—of which I won both games—and told me that Gloria is fine, although confused about her episode.

Tiredness makes my brain slow, and I blink and yawn. After a moment, I hear a scratching noise and realize that's what woke me up.

Tabby.

Embarrassed I've somehow forgotten about her, but reminding myself that she is quite capable of handling herself, I untangle myself and quietly go to the door to let her in.

Only deep dark shadows greet me in the hall, a smudge of a moon outside sending pale light through the window. The eerie family portrait across the way unnerves me, the eyes of a young Tallulah and her parents seem to watch me as I step onto the worn carpet. "Tabby," I call softly. "Is that you?"

Dead silence greets my ears, heavy enough to make my skin tingle with prickles of dread. I try the hall light switch, but the chandeliers overhead flicker and die.

This cat. She's as bad as my guardian angel.

Leaving the sisters asleep, I take a flashlight and search out the door at the other end of the hallway. It's unlocked, and a weak beam comes on when I push the tiny button on the old fashioned light switch inside.

The odor of old books and dried leather fill the air. It smells like this place hasn't been opened in decades. Dust coats every surface.

The room is as Kalina described, filled with bookshelves, a long wooden table reminiscent of a library, leather chairs, and three green-hooded banker's lamps. There are also several elegant ones with stained glass shades in various spots, and bronze statues on end tables and the mantel.

"Hi, Ava." Sherlock sits in a leather chair, reading a book.

The main conference table is stacked with newspapers and magazines. I turn on a banker's lamp and see a newspaper from the seventies on top of one stack. Others go back years before that. "Find anything interesting?" I ask the ghost.

"Tons! I wish I could take half the collection back to the library. Paris would love it."

Sherlock latched onto me at Christmas when I visited another town several miles away for a few witchy supplies. I ended up at the library next to the metaphysical shop, and Paris, the librarian, supplied me with some valuable information. She and her sister run an entire magical library underneath the mundane one, and Sherlock made that his home.

Fortunately, he decided to "take my case" at Christmas and hitched a ride home with me.

The papers are yellowed and brittle, fine motes rising from them as I browse through the dates. The dust coats my nose and makes me sneeze. "Excuse me." I sniffle and back away from the table. "Is Persephone your Dr. Watson now?" I tease him.

"If only." He looks a tad forlorn. "She's a difficult one, that guardian angel of yours."

"Tell me about it." I admire the handiwork of the fireplace. "You're sweet on her, aren't you?"

"You think I'd hang around and tolerate her bullying otherwise?"

"She's a pickle for sure, but don't give up. I think she gives you so much grief because she likes you."

His face brightens. "Truly?"

"Truly. Say, I never thanked you for helping with Sean O'Reilly. I appreciate what you did at the ball."

He straightens a bit. "No need for gratitude. That spirit was a mean one. I was happy to come to your aid."

"Any idea who killed Sal?"

"None, I'm afraid, but you'll figure it out. The players in this ruse are not all that clever, I assure you."

I'd like to believe him. At least he seems to want to help. "Were you alive during the twenties?"

"Ah, yes. I'm older than you think perhaps."

From what I've learned of him, he seems to believe he's Sherlock Holmes. "Of course. I forgot. You lived your heyday in the 1800s, correct?"

He tips his hat to me.

"Your favorite case, Mr. Holmes?"

His face turns pensive once more. "The lady asks a tough question. A Scandal in Bohemia, if you must know."

"THE woman, then?"

"You know my adventures?"

This game seems to bring him pleasure. Or maybe he's as unstable as some of the other ghosts I've encountered, and really does believe the illusion. Either way, he's charming and smart. "Doesn't everyone? Even those who haven't read them have heard of Irene Adler."

"A difficult woman, indeed."

"Seems you like the challenging ones."

He laughs. "They are always fun. They challenge my mind."

A cursory inventory of the shelved volumes leads me to a section of ledgers three rows back from where I stand. This corner of the room is dark, so I turn on my flashlight to read the gold lettering on the bindings.

Accounts dating back to the thirties, and below them, a row of guest registries. I grab those that correspond directly with the end of World War II and return to find Sherlock is gone. In his place, Tabby is seated on the table watching me.

Her golden eyes flash in the illumination. I click it off. "Where did you come from?"

She blinks and hops off a pile of faded magazines, sending the stacked issues to the floor.

"Nice." I set the registries on the seat of a chair and bend to pick them up. "Thanks a lot."

I flick on the beam again to see under the table better where several have slid to. It glances off a pale piece of wood.

At first, I think it's simply a chair leg, but these are all built from dark planks.

I re-stack the magazines and shine the light across the carpet once more, moving from my end to the far one. My breath catches.

The beam slides along curved handles, spindles, rails, and a seat. Hidden underneath the table is a child's rocking chair.

What is that doing here?

Even stranger is that there is another item concealed there, too.

Lying haphazardly on its side is the last thing I expect to see.

Discolored in the light, is the matching bridal shoe to Sal's murder weapon.

"You shouldn't be in here!"
Tallulah's voice rings out and makes me jump, bonking my head on the tabletop. "Ouch!"

Coming out of my crouch, I rub the injured spot and the shadowy room blurs. Blinking to clear my vision, I see her spectral body fly past, leaving a trail of ghostly cold in her wake.

The chill rolls over me like a wave. I grit my teeth and breathe deeply, attempting to slow my poor, skipping pulse.

"Is this yours?" I bend down and tug the rocking chair out, having to shift one of the bulky wooden seats aside in order to do it.

She whizzes past me again, disappearing amongst the rows of shelves. "Get out!"

She's so adamant, it makes me pause. "An unusual place to hide a child's rocking chair, isn't it?"

The voice comes from behind a bookshelf. "None of your business."

I stand still, mind searching for a subject to make a connection with her. I'm no mind reader, but I've found that establishing a relationship, even if it's brief, often helps me discover more about the spirit and, in turn, they feel more willing to trust me with their secrets. "Did you like to read?"

I don't know what happened in this hotel or why it's keeping her anchored here, but this is what I do. I try to help the ghosts in whatever way I can.

She peeks around the corner, and I mentally check myself so I don't startle. "Look, I'm not trying to invade your space, but you can't stay here for eternity. Your spirit needs to move on. I know it can be scary to cross to the afterlife, but—"

She zooms out from her hiding place to hover in front of me, her face bearing down close to mine. "You know *nothing*."

I explain that I actually do know a thing or two about the spirit world. "In fact, I've crossed over more than a few ghosts, and I can help you, too."

The silence of the old books and the dust on the lamps mocks me.

"Persephone? I could use some help here. Sherlock?"

I'm talking to thin air.

Tabby sits near the cracked open door, staring at me as though she's bored. I grab the registers—no sense in wasting my breath. Maybe if I can figure out who the man in the photo is, I'll have a better chance of securing the connection I need to encourage Tallulah to move on.

As I take a step toward the exit, the ghost appears again, and her face is contorted with rage. This time I do startle and step back— if she could get a hold of Gloria, she can do the same to me. "Jeez. Don't do that."

I've tangled with death a couple times already in my almost thirty years. I certainly don't plan to go out because of her, and Logan isn't here to bring me back from any near-death experience, as he has previously.

Twice.

I really should keep him around when dealing with ghosts.

The problem is, she's between me and my escape. "I've heard a baby's laughter and cooing, seen a lot of other ghosts as well." Maybe a distraction will work. "Why is that? There are so many spirits still tied to this place."

She seethes, but says nothing, continuing to float. Her fists flex and she looks like she's about to explode.

I shouldn't keep pushing, but I can't help it. She obviously needs to talk to someone, and since I'm the only ghost whisperer in the area, it seems I get to be her therapist as well. "What happened, Tallulah? Did the chair belong to someone else? The child I keep hearing, perhaps?"

She makes a noise in her throat that sounds like a dog growl. "It was mine. Now leave."

"Why did you attack my friend?"

She races away, turning toward the table. "She deserves to die. She should have never been born."

Tabby meows loudly and paws at the door. It's open enough for her to pass through it, so I ignore her. "Why would you say that? You don't even know Gloria."

"I know enough. It's not fair!"

Now we're getting somewhere. "What's not, Tallulah? If you tell me what's going on, I might be able set things straight."

A sob echoes through the room. "Why won't everyone leave me alone?"

"Are the ghosts bothering you?"

"Not them, the people!"

"They make me batty, too, but honestly, I can help you—"

"Ava?" The door opens fully, and Tabby darts out as Penn pops her head in. "Who are you talking to?"

I glance around. Tallulah is gone.

From the corner of my eye, I still see the shoe under the table. Who put it there? And why?

I decide to leave it for now. If the murderer believes

they've gotten away with something, I'll let them continue with that assumption.

"The cat," I reply, handing her the flashlight. The registers are growing heavier by the minute. "Come on, let's go back to the suite. You and Jenn better stay with me tonight."

And hopefully, Tallulah doesn't.

## 11

"What's going on?" Jenn asks, sleepy-eyed when we return. Tabby jumps on the back of the couch and stretches out. Jenn lazily strokes her fur.

"Nothing important." I wish I had some of Helen's peach wine as I rub my sore head. "You two take the twin beds in the master room."

In the kitchen, I set the registers on the table, and reach for the cold coffee. There's enough to fill a cup and I pop it into the microwave.

Penn enters and points at the stack of books. "Light reading before bed?"

I'm typically asleep way before midnight. "I'm looking for a connection between the previous owner and a man she may have had a crush on." I play it off like it's no big deal. "I'm a sucker for a good romance, and I believe their relationship might have been a secret. Fun to think about, anyway. A clandestine love affair is good inspiration for a new line of gowns."

"Ooh," Jenn says, pulling a chair from the table and plopping into it. Both look intrigued. "We can help."

"It's late. You should get some sleep. Tomorrow's a big day." For me as well, I don't add. "I'm only going through these briefly for a name that might be associated with him. That's all."

Penn returns to the living area and picks up the almost empty popcorn bowl. "I'm in."

"Me, too," Jenn agrees. She wiggles her fingers for the snack. "Where do we start?"

I guess it can't hurt. Once Penn's grabbed drinks for them, I hand each a registry. "I believe he was a war veteran, so we'll start with these. We're looking for the last name Monroe."

The leather binding of my ledger creaks as I open it. The slight odor of mold drifts up. It's dated 1946.

The penmanship of the scant handful of guests varies between elaborate flourishes and scrolls to impossible-to-decipher scribbles. It looks like a war between accomplished artists and three-year-olds.

The girls' enthusiasm wanes after an hour, and my frustration builds. We find no mention of anyone with that name, and there are another six volumes to search.

Jenn sits back and stretches. "My eyes are crossing. Maybe I do need some sleep."

Penn agrees, rubbing her eyes. "Me, too, I'm afraid."

"If I have time tomorrow, I'll keep looking," I stack the registers we've finished to one side. "Thanks for your help."

Jenn rises and glances around, stifling a yawn. "Did you guys find any secret rooms in this suite?"

Even with the coffee, my brain cells are fried and I give her a blank look, not comprehending. "Sorry, what?"

Penn hitches a thumb over her shoulder towards the connecting suites. "We found one in ours. Kind of disturbing, if you ask me."

I'm certainly curious and I wonder if Sherlock has already

discovered it. Old buildings like this are known for such things, so it's not entirely surprising.

From what I know about many of the south's plantations and farmhouses, people often hid heirlooms, gold, and other valuables from invading armies and criminals in them. Probably half the homes in this area were once a part of the Underground Railroad. "Why is it disturbing?"

Jenn places a hand on her belly, as if protecting her unborn child. "Do you want to see it? I think it's sad more than anything."

I follow the girls to the end suite. Faded rose wallpaper, honey oak furniture, and ivory lace curtains offer a more feminine and modest decor than in the main one.

Passing through the living area and into the bedroom, Tabby dashes between our feet. Penn presses the button on the wall switch, and two sconces cast pale, yellowy light onto a twin bed, sparse bookshelf, and a large trunk.

"They need air fresheners," she comments, waving a hand under her nose.

Jenn guides the trunk to one side. "I was trying to sleep last night, but the storm kept waking me up. It was so dark in here with no window, so I kept playing with the flashlight. That's when I saw the way the wallpaper had peeled away from this spot."

She touches an edge, lifting the frail paper near the trim board. Her fingers slide under it, gently peeling it back. "There's a metal latch here."

With a soft grunt, she gives a tug, and a section shifts and disappears.

A pocket door.

Jenn moves aside and motions me to step in. Penn hands me a flashlight from the dresser. "There are no lights in there."

As the thin illumination slides over the sparse furniture

and hidden remnants of Tallulah's life, a shiver slides down my spine. "I'm with you, Penn. This is full-on creepy."

It's indeed a hidden room, but not one full of valuables. At least not in the strictest sense. My mind tries to understand what it was used for and why.

Jenn yawns audibly and I retreat from the space, leaving it open. "Let's get you two to bed."

After the sisters are in the master bedroom asleep, and I've stopped my pulse from racing, I take a deep breath and sneak back to the secret room and its contents.

They create more questions than answers, and yet, I sense I'm getting closer to the latter. A bassinet, an adult-size rocking chair, and a chest of drawers add to the growing picture I have of Tallulah's past.

Steeling myself, I open the top drawer and find handmade baby clothes neatly folded. They appear unused. For a few minutes, I finger them, studying the items and trying to put some of the pieces together.

"What is this?" I murmur in the flat silence.

Tallulah appears next to me, sad and resigned. Her earlier anger has vanished. "Mine."

"Your what?"

"My sin." She glances at me, then away. "Now you know why I can't ever leave."

## ❧ 12 ❧

Frosty goosebumps race up and down my arms. "Tell me what happened."

Tallulah's spectral form is shedding icy waves of energy, and it's all I can do to keep my teeth from chattering.

"I did something bad," she says forlornly. "I'm doomed to go to hell."

My gaze travels to a rosary hanging on the back of the bassinet. Until now, I haven't paid attention to the scattered relics of religion in the personal wing. There are crosses on the walls here and there, more artsy than pious, and there's a family Bible in the parents' bedroom on the nightstand between the beds.

Earthbound spirits sometimes fear karma so much they attach themselves to this world like a tick on a dog. Fear is a compelling motivator and can give them the strength they need to stay anchored here.

"The other side isn't like that," I attempt to reassure her. "There's really not a hell, per se. Once you pass over, from what I understand, you go through a review of this lifetime and the lessons and challenges you experienced here."

She stares at me with deep-set, dark eyes, just like those in the family portrait. "I don't understand."

"Like in school when you got to the end of the year and took a test to review what you learned?"

Her face remains blank.

"In essence, you're given a deeper understanding of why you were here, and the opportunity to evaluate what you may have gotten wrong. The thing is, they're all lessons. Life isn't really about right and wrong, but learning and doing better when you know how. That way, the next time you incarnate, you hopefully fix any bad karma you built up and grow into a better human being."

"Karma? Reincarnation?"

"Surely you've heard of both."

"Of course I have, but that's not what Papa said."

I'm walking on eggshells now. "Look, I don't have all the answers, but I do know you don't have to fear crossing over. Have you seen a light by chance?"

She stares at me as if I've turned into Satan right in front of her eyes. "You're lying."

I raise a hand. "I swear on my Mama's manners—which are the best in the south—that I'm telling the truth."

"How is it you can see me?"

"I have a gift." I try not to cough or choke on the word. "I see spirits, and can interact with them sometimes."

"You've seen the other side? Heaven?"

Not exactly. "I've survived two near-death experiences. It gives me insight most folks don't have."

"Heaven is a real place?"

There's so much hope in her voice, I form my next words carefully. "It's a concept, and if you believe in it, it exists for you."

She narrows her eyes. "Then hell *is* real."

I shrug. "For some, I suppose. Most create their own

version of that here on earth."

Floating to the bassinet, she turns her back on me. "The innocent should go to heaven, even if they were never baptized, don't you think? He was only a baby."

Fear and grief are two of the strongest emotional anchors for spirits. Luckily, love tops them all.

The clothes in the dresser are neutral colors and hand-made with love. "You had a boy?"

Her hand flows through the fabric covered side of the bassinet, enough energy exuding from her fingers to make the rosary swing. "Papa was so angry. He said I couldn't tell anyone. We had to keep it a secret."

Dozens of questions fill my head. I wonder if I'm up for this—learning what I've wanted to know. Shifting my weight, I mentally reach for my guardian angel. For Sherlock. Even Aunt Willa. Heck, I'd take anyone who could give me courage at the moment.

No help comes and I take a deep breaths to steel myself. I ask the one question I fear the most. "What happened to the baby?"

She lifts her head as if she hears something far away. I strain my ears, but I don't pick up on anything. She slowly turns to me, face contorting with unshed tears and pent up grief. "Don't ever set foot in here again."

Poof, she's gone. I heave a sigh of frustration, but also relief. I hope her father isn't hanging around because I don't want to meet him. My words to him will not be as gentle.

Half-heartedly, I call out to her, ask another question, but a noiseless hush fills my ears.

Persephone appears in the rocking chair, seated. She's wearing a gauzy dress with rhinestone earrings dangling from her lobes. Her hair is styled with finger waves and is contained with a headband matching her jewelry. "Sad, isn't it?"

"Your timing needs work. Where have you been?"

"Listening."

"You didn't hear me mentally begging for your help?"

She studies me with a frown. "You don't need it. You need confidence."

Fine. Whatever. "Do you know what happened with the child?"

Her gaze on me is steady. "Do you?"

My brain cells are shutting down and I'm freezing. Ghosts are divas sometimes, but I can't blame Tallulah for her mood swings. My guardian angel, on the other hand, is a complete pain in my backside, and I don't feel sympathy for her. "Come on, Seph, do you know or not?"

She rocks, the vintage chair making squeaking noises. "You're making good progress. Keep at it. And make sure your friend, Gloria, doesn't return."

"Why?"

"You know I can't tell you everything. I can only guide."

I feel like throwing the flashlight at her, but I need to talk to someone about this. "Tallulah fell in love with a guest, didn't she? They had an affair, she became pregnant, and because it was out of wedlock, her father didn't like it. Something happened to the child."

Persephone waggles her hand in a fifty-fifty gesture. "Close, but it's her story to tell. She's never disclosed it to anyone. Once she works through it with you, she'll be ready to move on. This is part of the process for some of them, and it serves you, too. You're going to encounter this in the future, so pay attention. If Tallulah divulges her past to you, you'll understand far more of what's going on here."

I'm not sure I want to. "Cryptic, thanks. If that's all you've got, I'm going to bed."

It feels somewhat satisfying to slam the door on her.

## ❦ 13 ❦

Saturday morning arrives with the smell of brewing coffee, and Rosie's grandmother hovering over me as I wake up.

"Geez!" I startle, clutching the blanket to my chest.

"Ysela is a perfectly proper name for the baby," she insists, her face only inches from mine as she levitates. "I predicted this, you know!"

Ghosts have little concept of time or personal space. Best to play along with abuela or she'll add to my already too-full plate. "You did?"

"I told her she would have a girl. It was in the last reading I did."

Ysela Gomez-Estrada—Sela, to her friends—dropped dead of a heart attack at her psychic table at the Thorny Toad shortly after Thanksgiving. She'd had a bad ticker for years, according to Rosie, but the family was still shocked. Rosie always claimed she was too stubborn to do so and would probably outlive all of them.

I need caffeine in the worst way. "I'll give her your

message." I sit up, rub my eyes, and swing my feet around to the floor. "Now, can I have some privacy?"

After I clean up, I softly call for Tallulah. Then I try Monroe. I even reach out to the baby, but no dice. In fact, the ghosts are all eerily quiet, as the sisters and I head downstairs to start the biggest day of the fair.

We grab breakfast from the buffet in the dining room. Rosie and Gloria greet us at the booth when we're stuffed full.

Great. I need to deliver the message to Rosie, and Persephone told me to keep Gloria away.

"There's a long line outside already." Rosie bustles around, putting on her name tag and setting up the table for consultations.

I inquire how both she and Gloria feel this morning, and express that I'm a bit surprised my seamstress has returned after her experience.

Rosie waves me off, claiming she's fine, and Gloria pats my hand. "I wouldn't miss this for the world. Doc declared I'm healthy as can be."

As Rosie and the sisters re-drape fabric over our arches and adjust the potted plants, Victoria breezes by.

"Victoria?" Rosie calls. "Can we have a few more chairs?"

She barely glances our way, gives a nod, and keeps going.

Gloria scans the pillars in the room and some of the artwork with a smile on her face. "I just love the architectural details. I dreamed about this place last night." She squeezes my arm. "Plus, you're up to six dress orders. I bet today you get even more. I can't wait to swing into production!" A red and white tape measure hangs around her neck. "If I'm here, I can take the brides' measurements, and that will help speed up production."

I'm sure to Darinda, or any of the other bridal suppliers, that seems paltry. To me, it's everything.

"We're doing it," I say to Gloria, and secretly to my Aunt Willa, who I owe all of this to. The grin on my face can't be denied.

A young man with a camera bustles about, snapping pictures, and I see Victoria giving him instructions. He stops at our booth and asks if he can take a few to distribute to the local papers and online.

"Are you a wedding photographer?" I ask.

He nods. "I do freelance work."

I gather everyone near the sign with our business name, and Rosie slides a mannequin next to me. "Make sure to get the gown."

As he departs, Baldwin arrives with metal chairs. "Victoria said you needed these." He begins unfolding them, and Penn and Jenn arrange them near our table. "Sleep okay?"

He seems to brace himself, as if fearing I'll say no. I didn't rest much at all, but the poor fellow pulls at my heartstrings. It can't be easy to run a successful business that's haunted when you don't want it to be. He and his wife have been so gracious, and I appreciate that they tried to save the hotel. "Just fine, thank you. We enjoyed the popcorn."

Across the way, I notice Victoria, Darinda, and Christine huddled in conversation. They stare in our direction and seem to be zeroed in on me.

Detective Jones arrives, Kalina handing him a cup of coffee as she greets him and whizzes on by. She shoots a glance at Baldwin that seems like a warning, and he hastily leaves with a, "Have a good day" to us.

He hustles out after his wife. The group of women converge on Jones. He stands a head taller than all of them, and I receive scrutiny from him.

Victoria checks her watch and breaks away. It must be time to open. Darinda and Christine return to man their booth.

I casually arrange a floral pot next to my sign. "What's up?" I ask Darinda.

"Good morning to you, too."

I grab one of the seats and slide it around so we can get at least four people at the table. Some of the groups coming in have that and more. "Excuse my poor manners. Good morning."

"I was getting an update on Sal's murder." She motions at Christine to bring their business sign out front and center. "The detective told us there's bruising on the back of Sal's head that suggests he was knocked out by something hard." She motions to the base of her skull, lowering her voice. "He also had a jagged cut here. Not deep, but Detective Jones is looking for another weapon."

Something besides the shoe? That's interesting. Must be why Sal didn't have defensive wounds. Somebody bonked him, knocking him down. Then they used the heel to stab him. "Is it possible the killer was wearing the shoe?"

She shrugs.

It would make sense. They could've stomped on Sal's neck, driving the stiletto into it.

I scan my memory, trying to recall any item backstage that night that was both hard enough to render him unconscious, and that might have a sharp edge to cause the wound.

I come up blank. Darinda is working on a jewelry display, and I have to move closer to her booth. "Did they get DNA from the shoe?"

People begin to file in, conversation and laughter ringing through the room. She doesn't look at me, glancing toward the rush instead. "He didn't say. Sorry, Ava, but we must get busy."

The wave of brides descends on us. I'll have to continue my investigation later.

## ❧ 14 ❧

I take orders for five more gowns, and Gloria measures and sizes each woman as we go.

Rosie only has to dash off once for the restroom, and as we come up for air a few hours later, she grabs her water bottle and a bag of crackers from her purse. "We're nearly booked with consultations and events through fall. Can you believe it?"

Victoria has undoubtedly put on a successful fair for us, and I'm guessing for many of the other vendors as well. The management company she works for creates and runs these throughout the south. I imagine they're only going to get bigger and better every year.

It's been a good day, and it's not over yet. I see a text from Logan, and I call to tell him the good news. He offers congratulations and invites me to dinner.

I can tell by his voice and the fact he's hedging about where he's taking me that he has something up his sleeve. Since it's Valentine's, I presume it's a swanky venue. I agree to be ready for him to pick me up at seven, giving Rosie and me the chance to close and prep for our final day.

The enormity of that fact hits me all over again. I'm running out of time to help Tallulah, as well as figure out who killed Sal.

Using my phone, I do a search for her name. Her obituary is the first thing that pops up.

Gloria sits in a chair off to the side, looking as happy and tired as I am. She releases a big sigh. "Now I know why I've never attended one of these. That was an intense morning."

The obit doesn't mention any child, only her parents. I didn't expect it to. It does, however, mention the famous hotel.

I fall down the rabbit hole, searching for info on Emanuele. More about the hotel surfaces, including the history surrounding it. There are articles spanning a time-frame from the opening to Tallulah's death, and I'll have to save most to read later.

Of course, there are seasonal Halloween write-ups about the hauntings. The owners before Baldwin and Kalina made quite a big deal about it, claiming that's why they went bankrupt.

Gloria leans forward to read over my shoulder. "This place is a marvel. We should do a photoshoot here." She claps her hands. "It's perfect for your new line of flapper gowns."

"I guess so," I murmur, inwardly cringing at the idea of hanging out with the ghosts.

She stands, her focus a million miles away. "Have you walked through the courtyard? It's so upscale, and the grand stairs—we could showcase all the dresses at once on the various steps, then do individual pictures."

I chuckle at her enthusiasm. I'm not sure the reputation of a haunted hotel is what I want attached to my designs, but she's right about the building also having an unmistakable nostalgic atmosphere. "I'll speak to Baldwin and see if we can work something out. Outside of its reputation for being haunted, it actually could be a great destination wedding spot when you think about it. The Cross Vineyard is only five miles north, historic Thornhollow is within easy driving distance, and it's only a few hours to Atlanta."

Rosie nods. "That's actually a great idea for an investor who has the money. Unfortunately, I don't think Baldwin and Kalina do."

"I'd get married here," Jenn says. "I like the idea that it's haunted. I think they should do ghost tours and deck it out at Halloween."

"My father always told me to respect history and learn from it," Gloria says, suggesting ghost tours are ridiculous. "I credit him for my love of old buildings. He sure would have gawked at the ornamentation here. Always had an eye for details when it came to architecture."

Persephone pops in behind Gloria and points to her as the seamstress resumes her seat. I fumble around for a couple seconds, trying to understand my guardian angel's antics and then my mind clicks. "Is your dad still alive?"

"I'm sorry to say he's not. He passed some years ago. He was wounded in the Second World War, and the doctors couldn't get all the shrapnel from his chest. I guess it finally moved the wrong way. I miss him every day."

We offer condolences, and she looks wistfully at the nearby mannequin wearing the Ella dress. "That's how he met my mother. She was a nurse in France and secretly part of the Resistance. They fell in love, but he was an American spy. Can you believe it? She didn't know that about him, and he didn't know her activities either. What a pair, all those secrets." She tsks. "He couldn't tell anyone his real name, and he was ordered home as soon as he was able to walk after his injuries healed. He thought he'd return to Paris once the war was over and find her, but when it ended, he had...issues. You know?" She makes a whirling motion with one finger at her temple. "I think he figured she was better off without him, so he didn't contact her."

"You mean... What did your mom call it?" Jenn asks me. "Shell shock?"

All kinds of connections are forming in my head. "Yes. PTSD."

Penn and Jenn are fascinated, listening intently. "How did they end up together then?" Penn asks.

"She didn't have his actual name, but she hunted him down." Gloria laughs. "It took her nearly two years, but she did it. That's my mother for you. Tenacious."

Sounds like mine. "Did your dad ever visit this place to recover? Mama said there were men who did."

Her brow furrows. "He never talked about the war or any of his life before he married *ma mere*. He kept it bottled up. Mama always said he suffered from the memories. Had nightmares. Things like fireworks could send him into a terrible state. My brother and I would sometimes hear him roaming the house at night, unable to sleep, but we weren't allowed to talk about it. Not a word! He needed help, but I don't believe he ever got any."

I decide to look at the registries again, just to see if I can find his name. My sixth sense is tingling, and Persephone is still giving me the eye, as though there's something important here. This must tie in with Tallulah. "But he did come here when he returned to the States, right?"

She tilts her head, curious at the question. "Yes, he was too mentally off to continue as a spy. Mother mentioned once it was good he had carpentry skills. He could build anything with his hands. Such craftsmanship. He never had a steady job, though, always moving from one project to another."

"Is that why you like to work with your hands?" Jenn asks.

Gloria smiles. "Probably. My father passed his talents on to me."

I smooth the tablecloth. "What was your dad's name?"

Curiosity dances in her eyes. "Abe."

"And the last ?"

She gives me a confused smile. "Romone, why?"

A part of me wonders if that was his real name. Being a spy couldn't have been easy. Deflated, I show her the photo on my phone of Tallulah's mystery fellow. "Have you ever seen this man?"

Gloria peers at the screen, scrutinizing it. "Oh my."

At that moment, Victoria enters the booth. "Ava, it's time."

"For what?"

She taps her pen against her clipboard. "Tell me you didn't forget."

I'm lost. "Forget what?"

She grabs my arm and hauls me out of the chair. "You're giving a speech!"

## ❧ 15 ❧

I try to get out of it, I do
Victoria won't let me. "There are at least a hundred brides in there," she says, brushing non-existent dust from my sleeve. "It's standing room only, and you're already late."

Rosie and the sisters smile at each other. Gloria continues to study the picture. "But I..."

"Did you get any sleep last night? You look like death warmed over."

"Thanks, Mama," I grouse.

"Excuse me?"

"Nothing. Look, I'm not prepared." I point to our dwindling stack of flyers listing our services. "I can hand out business cards and service info."

"Don't be ridiculous. They didn't buy tickets and pack the conference room for that. They want to learn something, feel inspired."

Before I can argue, she grabs my wrist and tugs me forward. Over my shoulder, I look at Rosie. "Help?"

"You've got this." She gives me a thumbs-up.

Fine manager she is.

I call to Gloria, "We'll continue this when I get back."

She continues to stare at the screen. Rosie waves me off. Penn and Jenn rise and go running past us. "We want to hear your speech," Penn calls, both of them giggling as they bump into folks and hustle out.

I plant my feet and nearly jerk Victoria to a stop. "Can't someone else do it?" I point at the Southern Bride tent. "I bet Darinda would love to, and you said you could find one of the big city vendors to replace that other gal."

"You didn't want them to do it previously."

"A lot has happened since then." And I'm totally unprepared. "Darinda's great at this stuff."

Victoria keeps her grip on me, her fingers biting into my skin. "She's already scheduled for three. It's you, then Just Say Yes Jewelry, then Southern Bride. Now come on."

She pulls, I resist. "I don't want to."

"You have to."

A tug-of-war ensues.

Brides and their party members begin to gather. "You're making a scene," she hisses.

"Me? You're attempting to bully me into doing something I don't want to do."

A woman holds a booklet from a vendor to her lips and says something behind it to her friend. Another holds up her phone to film us.

Mama will kill me if this ends up on YouTube.

I stop fighting her and we nearly topple over. "Fine," I say. "I'll do it."

Victoria releases me and straightens her black blazer. "Good." She raises her chin and tucks her clipboard under her arm. "Let's go."

Outside the ballroom, I take a deep breath, my mind scrambling for something to talk about in front of a hundred brides.

Down the hall, past the bar, we come to a halt outside the door to the conference room. My nerves are buzzing. "What is it I'm supposed to discuss again?"

She looks like she's going to skin me alive. "Your theme is Finding Your Fantasy Gown, remember?"

"Right, okay." That shouldn't be hard. I can come up with a few pointers, and maybe land a few orders in the process. "Um, how long should I speak?"

I swear steam comes out her ears. "Sixty. Minutes."

My stomach flips over. "You're saying I need to talk for a *full hour?*"

"This could be a boon for you and your new line."

"I'm sorry, but you need to find someone else. This just... I'm not..."

She takes my arm and squeezes as if she's going to force me inside. With her determination, I'm not sure I can hold her off. "You spoke quite eloquently the other night on stage in front of all of these people plus more. Do it again."

"Yeah, but that was spontaneous, and I was talking about my gowns and my personal philosophy on weddings. Plus, it was all of, like, ten minutes."

Her eyes go squinty. "Do you want me to inform all the women in that room you're under suspicion for murder?"

I gasp in a breath. Blackmail? Okay then, I see how it is. "Well, bless your heart. Aren't you manipulative? You know I'm innocent."

"Actually," she says with an evil smile, "I don't know any such thing."

Hardball. Fine. "I'll give the speech, but I want top billing at next year's event."

I see the wheels spin in her head. "If you're not in prison, I'll see what I can do."

Derision to boot. "Would you like some pepper with that salt?"

"Huh?"

"Never mind." I extend my hand.

We shake on it, and she pushes the French doors open. I follow her in and smile as she introduces me.

The clapping is loud enough to make me reassess my fear of public speaking. Some of them attended the runway show and heard my approach to making your day special. Most look captivated by what I'm about to say.

My mind drifts to my fantasy gown. How it will feel to wear it at my wedding to Logan.

*If* I get married.

Someday, I bolster myself, finding Penn and Jenn toward the back and seeing their smiles.

The gown of your dreams is an integral part of most weddings. Some spend years in search of the Holy Grail. A few never find theirs, but most do, and it's pretty cool to see a bride-to-be's face light up when she finds "the one."

"Finding your fantasy gown," I say, taking over. The applause dies down and I have a rapt audience. "The most fun and important part of your whole wedding experience."

Persephone appears near the rear exit and gives me a wink.

At the same moment, I notice Victoria slipping out.

*Well, here goes nothing.*

## 𝕯 16 𝕰

"Where did you find that old photo?" It's the first thing Gloria asks when I locate her in the atrium later. She's staring at a beautiful hibiscus, but her expression is far away, as if she's remembering her dad.

"You recognize him, don't you?"

A slight mist clouds her eyes. She hands me the phone and nods. "I swear that's him, but..."

A few ladies from the conference room filter by. One tells me how much she enjoyed my talk. It seemed to go over well, many of the crowd stopping me before I could leave to ask me about consultations. I spent a good twenty minutes chatting with various brides, leading them to the booth so Rosie could take over to sign them up.

Now it's time for me to get back to business. The ghost business. "He sure was a handsome guy." I suspect the man wasn't a guest at the hotel, but I don't want to tell Gloria that he and Tallulah's lover are one and the same until I have proof. "I was doing research and came across it. Something in his features reminded me of you."

An exaggeration but it sounds plausible.

We're interrupted by a bride-to-be wanting to know about the Bellamy. I excuse myself from Gloria, and I chat about it as I walk her to the Enchanted Events booth. Gloria follows.

Rosie is finishing with the last client in line. It only takes a minute for the bride with me to declare she wants to order. Rosie takes her information and Gloria begins to measure her for it.

I sneak away and find Kalina at the front desk. "Do you have any old employee records?"

She barely glances up, typing away on the computer. "What do you want with those?"

"I'm still tracking down the man in the photo."

She sighs as if reaching for patience. "If there are, they must be in the study with the others. We only have the ones for the last couple of years here in the office."

"Thanks."

In the third floor study, I think about the shoe under the table while searching. Once again, dust flies as I dig through shelf after shelf, but come up empty-handed. Tabby makes an appearance, jumping on a velvet-covered reading chair near the fireplace and curling into a ball.

Sherlock materializes in the other, pipe in hand. "I hear you're having great success."

"Selling gowns, yes. Solving mysteries, not so much."

"You must consider every plausible possibility, and those that seem implausible as well."

Frustrated, I lean against a bookshelf. I need a shower and twelve hours of uninterrupted sleep. As Tabby snoozes, I'm actually jealous of her.

I stare at the table piled high with newspapers and magazines.

"Suppose she was wearing the shoes when she killed Sal." I pace the floor. "There would've been blood splatter on them and the clothes she wore that night."

"Assuming it's a female."

"Sal was the only man backstage, Baldwin was announcing the models. Do you know differently?"

"No, but it's possible a male entered the rear stage area while you were *chasing your cat*."

He smiles benignly over the lie.

"True. I can't rule it out a hundred percent, but my gut says it's a woman."

He simply nods and puffs on his pipe.

I continue to think out loud. "Was the killer a model? Could her gown still be here on a mannequin or possibly hidden in a vendor's booth?"

Sherlock stares at the fireplace as if there's a fire there. "Possibly. What else?"

"I still like Christine for it." I explain why and he makes noncommittal noises. "It might be prudent to check the Southern Bride space after everyone leaves tonight."

"Good idea."

I get down on hands and knees to check if the shoe is still there. It is. "Why hide the match to the murder weapon under here?"

"Plausible reason? Because it somehow implicates the killer."

"Right. And the implausible?"

He looks at me. "Because it implicates *a* killer."

"Not sure I understand."

He pockets his pipe and rises, giving Tabby a pat on her head. She yawns but doesn't open her eyes. "Perhaps our murderer wants to point the finger—or shoe, in this case—at someone else."

Who would they frame for it? He vanishes and I decide to not only check Southern Bride's booth, but to look at all the displayed dresses downstairs.

After washing my face in my suite's bathroom and putting

on a touch of lip gloss, I take the elevator down and find that evening has arrived.

Rosie is packing to leave. "Matt is picking me up for a Valentine's dinner. We're dropping Gloria at her house on the way."

I can see in Gloria's eyes that she has more questions, but before she can ask, I put my arm through Rosie's and pull her out of earshot. "We need to talk about your grandmother," I tell her.

"Abuela?"

I nod. "She wants you to name the baby after her."

"She's here?" Exasperation mixes with surprise. "Can she hear me right now?"

"She's not in the vicinity." I glance around and hope that's true. "But she seems quite fixated on you naming the child Ysela."

"Ha!" Rosie's raised voice draws more than a few people's attention. "First of all, we don't know if it's a girl or boy."

Persephone floats by like a balloon and says, "It's a girl."

I press my lips together, refusing to blow the surprise. Rosie knows me well, however.

"It's a girl? You're sure?"

I adamantly shake my head. "I have no insight into the sex of the baby. All I'm doing is passing on a message. You have free will and can name the child whatever you choose."

*Please make it something abuela can live with—no pun intended —because otherwise she will haunt me for the rest of my days.*

Rosie puts her arms around me and hugs me. "I'm sorry she's bugging you. It's not that I hate the name, but, well, it's so old-fashioned, you know?"

I'm prepared for this. Pulling out a napkin I scribbled down nicknames on, I hand it to her. "So modernize it. Change the Y to an I and call her Isi, or Lissi. Or choose a variant, like Iselina. That's my favorite."

"Iselina." She tries it out, accepting the list. "I like that. Wonder what abuela thinks?"

She looks at me expectantly. "Sorry, she's still not here at the moment."

"That's okay. It's our decision anyway. I'll speak to Matt."

"I figured you might. Enjoy your night."

Gloria tells me we'll talk tomorrow before she walks off with Rosie, arm in arm.

Logan arrives with a picnic basket. He greets me with a kiss. "Ready?"

I eye the basket. "I take it we're not going out?"

He slides his hand into mine, lacing our fingers together, and leads me from the ballroom. "I thought we'd eat in the atrium."

Most of the brides are off to enjoy the Saturday night dinner specials or to leave and go home. The vendors are packing up and heading for the dining room, too.

Not exactly what I'd expected, and I'm a little disappointed. I could use a break from the hotel, but I can hardly say no after he's gone to all this trouble.

Logan has planned well. He leads me to a small café table and two chairs with a flickering candle and flowers set up for us near the large glass display windows in the west.

The last of the sun sinks beneath the horizon, sending rays of peach and purple across the rolling lawn and down to the lake in the distance.

I slide into the chair, dropping my head into my hands. The past couple days are catching up on me. My lack of sleep is as well. I'd give anything to go home and spend the night in my bed, but I have no choice but to stay and figure out how to help Tallulah. I tell myself I'll rest up next week after the fair is over.

When I look up, Logan is frowning with concern. "This was a bad idea, wasn't it?"

I feel like the pin that has burst his balloon. I try to cover, smiling brightly. "Are you kidding? It's perfect. A beautiful location for our Valentine's Day dinner." I motion out the window at the setting sun.

He withdraws a bottle of champagne. Dom Perignon. "Brut Rose. Vintage 2006," he says with a grin.

That probably costs more than the rent on my old apartment. Two glasses come next, then he pops the cork.

A man and a woman—no doubt bride and groom—two rows over talk softly amongst the blooming plants, the bride catching my eye and smiling. Another couple chuckle and clap before they exit, the lady giving me a wink.

"How was today?" he asks as he pours.

I settle back into the chair and accept the glass he hands me, enjoying the way the fizzy bubbles tickle my nose. Champagne is definitely better than dust. "I think one of the original owners of this place had an affair with a man who used to work here."

Logan hesitates a brief moment before finishing pouring his own drink. He offers a toast. "To us."

I clink my pretty flute against his and sip. "To us."

He continues to unpack, hauling out an impressive array of food. "Queenie made your favorites."

My stomach rumbles, but my mind is elsewhere. I barely register the appetizers he sets on my plate. "I think that man is Gloria's father."

"Wow, that would be weird." He hands me a napkin. "I propose a toast."

"I thought you already did."

He grins and raises his glass, and it takes me a couple of seconds to realize that I need to shift gears and focus on him. I lift mine as well.

"To our future. I love you, Ava. Happy Valentine's Day."

"I love you too." A clink of our glasses. "Happy Valentine's Day."

Logan digs into his food. The champagne hits my system, and I know I need to eat, so I take a bite of an appetizer. It's delicious, but I still can't get my mind off how to break the news to Gloria about her dad and Tallulah. I have no proof, but I'm assuming—perhaps irrationally—that Tallulah's child may also be his.

"So, the fair is going well?" Logan finishes chewing and smiles.

"Yes, so far." Except for the fact that Sal was murdered and the killer hasn't been caught.

"I heard your speech today was a smash."

I shrug. "I wasn't prepared, so I had to wing it."

"These are kind of a big deal, aren't they?"

"For sure. The group that runs them, Top Event Management, has been doing them for years all over the country. It's a lot of business for them, as well as the vendors who attend."

"Between this and your wedding gown line, I suspect you'll need to expand next year. Hire another employee or two. Buy or lease a larger building. I've been looking at some that are on the market. After this is done, maybe we can go see them."

"Real estate? Employees? That's a big step."

"You're ready for it."

Am I? He wants to talk about the future, which is an excellent thing. Unfortunately, I'm sort of stuck in the past.

"It does appear that we may be able to expand Aunt Willa's business and even take it in a few new directions." I rub my forehead. "My mind is overwhelmed just thinking about it, even though I'm happy all this is happening."

We continue to chat, Logan talking more about future plans, including some together. "We better take that getaway we've been talking about before you get into the summer wedding season."

We've been considering several retreats for couples, but between our work schedules, we haven't had time to actually plan one and set aside a weekend for each other. I know it's important, but all I can do is nod and eat. "We definitely have to look at our calendars to figure out a date."

We finish the main meal. Logan pulls out a white box wrapped with a ribbon. "Queenie made your favorite cheese-cake for dessert."

I help him move the dirty dishes out of the way, taking a moment to smell the roses that are on the table in the beautiful display. Logan put a lot of work into this. I need to enjoy it and appreciate him. "You are both very thoughtful. This is just perfect."

It's dark outside now. Stars in the sky reflect off the lake. I haven't actually taken time to appreciate this peaceful setting since I've been at the hotel. I see now how it might be a restful retreat for someone recovering from the war or many of today's situations.

"This could be a resort again if they could find an influx of cash to fix it up and repair it."

Logan agrees. "I'm sure I could find investors who'd be interested. It's definitely a historical landmark. A great place for celebrations, parties, and..."

For me, it may always be a haunted hotel, but for others, it could be a beautiful, relaxing place to get away from the world. "And what?"

Logan refills my glass. I wonder if I should have more since I'm already feeling the effects.

"And other special occasions." He comes to my side and goes down on one knee next to my chair.

My stomach teeters. *What's he doing?*

I know exactly what.

Totally unprepared, my hands begin to shake. I set down the glass. Tabby appears across the way, watching us with interest. Or maybe hoping to score some leftovers. "What is this?"

His smile is the best thing I've seen all day. He withdraws a tiny blue box from inside his blazer.

An unseen person, probably Kalina, turns on soft overhead lights, illuminating the luscious plants all around us and spotlighting our table. Over Logan's shoulder, light glints off metal, drawing my eye. Tabby is now on a display of African violets. The trowel I used on Tallulah is lying next to one.

"Ava Fantome, you're the best thing that's ever happened to me." Logan takes my hand and squeezes it. "I've been in love with you from the day you returned to Thornhollow. These last few months have been the best of my life."

My gaze flicks to the tool. I can't help it. Tabby paws it and meows. A message? Warning?

It's flat. It has a sharp edge. Is this the weapon Detective Jones is searching for?

"I love you, too, Logan." *Forget the trowel.* I force my gaze back to his. His blue eyes mesmerize me. "I have since the fifth grade."

He chuckles softly and releases me to flip open the lid.

Just as he's about to propose, another thought enters my head.

*Not only is it the right type of weapon, it has my fingerprints all over it.*

## 𝕏 17 𝕏

"Hold that thought."

Logan's smile fades like melting ice cream. "What?"

"I'm so sorry, but I think someone may be trying to frame me for Sal's murder," I blurt.

Not exactly the reaction he was looking for. He snaps the box shut and stands. "This all went so much differently in my head."

Rising from my seat, I hug him. "I know, it's just—I want us to do this. The whole thing—dinner, the champagne, the ring, all of it, but there's a ghost here who wants to harm Gloria, and a living being who offed Sal and wants me to take the fall."

He sighs, the sound seeming to come from his toes. "Ava, have you had any sleep?"

His tone sounds a bit too much like Mama's. "I'm fine." Except for the ghosts and the fact I could end up in jail.

He lowers his voice and looks around. "You really think someone's setting you up?"

My scattered brain thinks through the logic of it, and

maybe it is a bit farfetched. How would the killer know I'd touch the trowel? That was totally spontaneous, and completely unlikely.

I try to reign in the drama. "Sorry. Maybe I do need more rest. Blame my mother for my overactive imagination, but I really must figure out who murdered Sal before Jones arrests me. You said yesterday that he doesn't have anyone else who looks good for it, and my alibi is weak." I tell him about the hit to Sal's head and the cut the weapon left behind. "I think I know what the killer used, and it just happens to have my fingerprints on it."

I point to Tabby and the trowel.

Logan stares at it a moment, and finally gives an exasperated nod. "How can I help?"

"Outside of wiping it clean?"

It's meant as a joke but Logan isn't playing along. "Seriously, Ava. Could someone be pointing at you for this?"

I eye the trowel over on the plant stand. "Regardless, why leave that in plain sight if he or she did use it?"

Tabby jumps down and strolls away. Logan takes a drink. "Why would they frame you?"

"Because of my charming personality?" Again, my attempt at humor falls flat. I know what he's getting at. "To take the spotlight off them."

He tilts his glass at me. "Exactly. You're a convenient suspect, not one they're out to get."

"I guess that makes me feel a little better."

"There was a generous amount of blood. They had to get some splatter on them. Better make sure no one's planted any bloody clothes or the other shoe on you."

There are at least fifty rooms where they could have hidden blood-stained clothes. If he or she is actually framing me, though, Logan's correct—I need to make sure there's no other evidence implicating me.

*Why hide that matching shoe in the study?*

Another question emerges that might answer that.

Who sent me there, where my fingerprints are now all over the door handle and table?

I stand. "Where's Kalina?"

Logan looks toward the entrance. "She helped me plan tonight, but I haven't seen her since I got here. It was Baldwin who showed me how she'd set up the table." He points at the flowers.

I haven't seen her since earlier either. "Kalina has access to all the rooms and suites."

"Yeah, so?"

I grab my phone and text Penn. "Come with me."

"What about dessert?"

I purse my lips, eyeing the bakery box. No sense passing that up. "Bring it with us."

We meet up with Penn and Jenn in the original ballroom. Only half the chandeliers come on when I hit the switch, and the spacious open-air room echoes with our footsteps as I lead the others to the runway. The backstage is still taped off.

The ghosts are enjoying a party, one that looks like its straight out of the 1920s. Women in flapper dresses dance with tuxedoed partners. Champagne flows, cigars burn. Under other circumstances, I might enjoy the show, sketch a few ideas.

"What's up?" Penn asks, bringing me out of the phantom *mise en scene.*

Logan sets the box on the raised stage. I motion for each of them to grab a piece of the luscious dessert. "Help yourselves while I pick your brains. This is the best chocolate cheesecake in three counties."

Logan had the sense to bring napkins, and we use our fingers to each select a piece. It's messy, but the dessert is extra thick and the pastry crust holds together nicely.

I explain my concern about being an easy target for Jones when it comes to the murder. "I need to know everything about that night. Do you remember where you were when you watched the last part of the runway show?"

Jenn points. "Over there. The seats were filled, so we had to stand along the wall."

"I sat a few rows back on the left with your mom and Queenie," Logan tells me.

I picture it in my mind. "The models came out in what order for Southern Bride?"

Penn licks whipped cream from her thumb. "Cathi, Christine, and Darinda."

"Cathi?"

"She works in the office," Jenn says. "We sort of hit it off backstage. She's Christine's younger sister. You've seen her."

I comb my memory and recall a short blond with a crooked front tooth and a penchant for bling. "Did she have any terse interactions or arguments with Sal?"

The sisters share a look and shake their heads in unison.

I can't remember seeing this Cathi at their booth, but maybe she was only here for the runway show. "Darinda modeled a dress?"

Both of them nod.

I'm not totally surprised. The two of us loved trying on sample dresses after hours. Plus, she's a beautiful woman with gorgeous curves, and has plenty of older brides as customers. "Did they each come out multiple times in the same order?"

Another dual nod. Good thing I'm not drunk or I'd be seasick watching the synchronized movements.

"Why?" Logan asks.

"Whoever killed Sal was backstage with him, that's a given, and I believe it's someone he knew. Maybe well. He never expected they would attack, and he was totally taken off guard."

Jenn's eyes widen. "You think he was murdered by Darinda?"

"Not her, but..." I stew and eat a bite of chocolate and whipped cream, studying the stage and attempting to recreate the timeline of what happened out here versus back there. "So Baldwin and Victoria were on stage announcing—"

"Victoria wasn't," Penn interrupts.

"She wasn't?"

Jenn swallows, shielding her lips with her fingers. "Not for the whole thing. She chased Tabby off the stage about halfway through the Southern Bride presentation. They ducked behind the curtain and she didn't return. I saw her later at the double doors when folks were leaving."

Did she tell Jones this?

"Yeah, but she was flirting with Sal before the show ever started," Penn states. "She seemed sweet on him. She wouldn't kill him."

Hmm. "How exactly did Sal respond to her attention?"

"He loved it." This from Penn.

"Like the diva he was," Jenn adds and they laugh.

No surprise there. These two barely knew him and yet picked up on his personality. "Did he reciprocate?"

Penn pauses. "I don't know if I'd call it that. I saw them a couple times that day and they seemed friendly, but that night, he was standoffish. I figured he was stressed about the show. I did overhear him say something regarding reporting her. At least, I think that's what he said. It was so noisy back there, it was hard to hear much of anything."

I stop eating. "Reporting her? For what? To whom?"

She finishes her piece, shaking her head. "Like I said, it was noisy, and I'm not sure what they were talking about. She seemed upset, though. She stopped flirting, that's for sure."

"There were several hundred people here that night,"

Logan reminds me, "and anyone could've walked backstage. It wasn't exactly a secured area."

"True, but I think the killer may have in-depth knowledge of this hotel, and that person had a relationship with Sal. Death by stiletto is a crime of passion, as my dad would say. Since it was a wedding shoe and that was Sal's bread and butter, it reeks of poetic justice."

Jenn brightens. "Like a statement. Revenge, maybe?"

"Could be." I polish off my slice. "If we figure out the motive, we can find the killer."

As we mull this over, the door to the room flies open. Victoria strides in, making a flabbergasted noise. "What in the world are you all doing in here?"

## ❧ 18 ❧

As she marches toward us, I wipe my hand on a napkin and swallow the last bite. "The night of the show, you chased Tabby from the runway, and you didn't return, is that correct?"

Her clipboard taps against her leg, impatient. This is a wooden one, like we used in school, not the metal document case she had when we checked in. "That cat!" Her face contorts as though she's sucked on a lemon. "Why in the world would you bring it and let her run loose? The hotel doesn't even allow pets."

I've worn the same expression more than a time or two. "Where did you end up once you ran her off?"

She eyes me as if I've grown a horn or two. "She went traipsing up onto the catwalk—I wasn't about to follow her up there. Crazy animal."

A charged look from her suggests that the crazy cat has a crazy owner as well.

I glance at the area above the stage, not having paid any attention to it previously. In my opinion, Tabby is a smart feline to go up there to get away from her. "Why didn't you return to the stage with Baldwin to introduce the last of the models and do the wrap-up?"

Her lips press together, eyes shuttering. Then she throws her hands up, the clipboard slapping her thigh when it comes down. "Fine, you caught me."

She sighs, and her shoulders slump. I notice her grip has made her knuckles white.

"With what?" Is she about to confess?

"Honestly, I needed a drink—a stiff one, if you know what I mean. I snuck off to the bar and snagged some schnapps. I took the bottle to my room then came right back so I could be here when the crowd let out."

Convenient, since the bar was closed. No witnesses there. "Did you tell Detective Jones?"

She touches the pen secured at her ear. "No, but I did square it up with Kalina and Baldwin. It's paid for."

Misdirection, my father would say, focusing on the stolen goods rather than her whereabouts. "Kalina saw you crossing between the backstage and the bar?"

"Of course. She was at the front desk."

Maybe she does have a witness. I make a mental note to verify this with our hostess. "Did you see anyone coming or going from the atrium while you were traipsing around?"

Her face takes on the *you're crazy* look again. "The atrium? No. I saw the photographer and that young Southern Bride model talking in the lobby. She was still in one of the dresses, which I thought was odd. Baldwin and Kalina were having trouble keeping the floor mopped from people tramping in with muddy shoes, thanks to the storm. The dress was going to get dirty. I doubted Darinda would appreciate that."

My mind flashes to my own gown and the dirty hem. Was it Cathi? "The photographer was taking a publicity shot?"

"I really couldn't say, but I doubt it. They seemed to be arguing."

How did they fit into this puzzle? "Do you use him at all your events? Do you have his contact info?"

"Not every one, but quite a few in Georgia. Some of the larger venues promote him for wedding photography but he prefers smaller ones like this. And of course I have his info, but it's in my...other clipboard."

"You sure are organized," Penn states.

Victoria barely acknowledges her. "Top Events Management is a million-dollar business. Organization is key to its fairs. Now, y'all need to leave this room."

Turning on her heel, she marches out. We toss the box. "Wonder if I should get on the catwalk?" I muse.

Logan eyes it and then me. "I don't think that's wise, and what would that tell you?"

Maybe that my shapeshifting great-great-grandmother witnessed the murder.

Instead of climbing up there and risking my neck, I should try talking to her. "Never mind. Victoria's right. Let's get out of here before Jones accuses me of tampering with the crime scene."

As we're exiting, Penn sidles up to me. "BJ's coming to get me. I think he's taking me out for Valentine's Day, but he says it's a big secret. He won't tell me the details. Jenn's coming, too. Will you need us tomorrow?"

I'm almost sad they won't be here tonight. "It's been good of you to help. I appreciate it. Enjoy a romantic night with your hubby. We'll talk soon, okay? No need for you to come back."

Each girl hugs me before they leave. Logan and I stroll through the large foyer. I see Darinda talking to Baldwin at the desk.

She glances over as we approach. There are bags under her eyes as pronounced as mine. Her usually perfect hair is a tad messy. A large tote bag is on her arm. "Are you staying again?" she queries.

My fantasy of going home and sleeping in my own bed hovers in front of me like a ghost. "I think I might. I rather like it here."

She doesn't know I'm lying. "See you tomorrow, then." She says goodnight to Baldwin and heads for the door. I fall into step with her, leaving Logan leaning on the desk. "Can I ask you a question?"

She digs in the tote and brings out a set of keys. "Sure, what is it?"

"How well do you know Cathi?"

She pauses, facing me. "Is she causing problems?"

Interesting that she'd jump to that conclusion. "Remember how much fun we used to have when the new lines came in? How we'd try them on after-hours playing the part of the bride?"

We always said it was for research. In essence, we were playing dress-up.

She smiles. "I miss those days."

"Me, too. Do you still do that with any of the other girls, like Christine or Cathi?"

She chuckles. "Heavens no. Christine is just an employee, not a friend."

"And her sister?"

"The only reason Cathi's still around is that she's fantastic with our social media and has mad computer skills."

"You've had issues with her?"

Darinda hesitates, glancing around, but then nods. "She's young. She makes mistakes."

"I know I sound nosy, but what kind? You mean, like, computer stuff?"

She fiddles with her keys as if deciding whether to answer.

"It's no big deal. She was using her break to try on gowns. I know some of the girls do it behind my back, but if she had just asked, I would have been happy to let her do it once in a while. One day, she forgot her phone in her car and left the building with a dress on. Not a sample, mind you, one a bride had already purchased and was waiting for alterations on. The dress hem became soiled. I was livid when I found out. Sal, too. As I said, it was a foolish mistake on her part. I reprimanded her."

"Sal wanted to fire her, didn't he?"

"You know how he is—*was*. But she's a wiz with so many things. She handles our website and designs these amazing ads. Our online sales have doubled since I hired her."

"The photographer who was taking publicity shots—has he done any shoots for you?"

"Jason? Sure, many times. Cathi recommended him. In fact, he's quite good."

I think about Victoria's metal document case, Jason's camera, and the trowel. All hard enough to do damage if swung at someone's head. The clip on the case and the lens on the camera have edges that could possibly break skin, much like the edges of the trowel.

"Thank you," I say, turning back to Logan. "See you tomorrow."

## ❧ 19 ❧

"You have that look in your eye," Logan says under his breath.

I watch Darinda through the glass entrance as she leaves. "What look?"

He threads his fingers through mine. We stroll past the once luxurious waiting area filled with antique chairs, elaborately molded side tables, and gold-framed pictures of landscapes that seem tired. "The one that says I'm not cuddling with you on the couch at my place tonight."

I grin. "You wanted to do more than that."

He winks.

"Are you checking out of the suite tonight, Miss Fantome?" Kalina carries a potted African violet to the desk where Baldwin sits doing a crossword puzzle.

The plant is in full bloom, probably fresh from the atrium. She's wearing gardening gloves and removes them as she speaks. "We have the Sweetheart Saturday event going on in the dining area if you and Mr. Cross want to attend."

I see her eye my finger for the engagement ring that's still in the box in Logan's pocket. "I saw it on the ad for the fair. Sounds fun."

"We have chocolates and a delightful drink list of Valentine cocktails. My favorite is the Love Potion martini. Raspberry and chocolate."

Logan meets my eye. "You want to stay, don't you?"

I bite my bottom lip, debating if there's any way I can make him happy and resolve both Tallulah's dilemma and Sal's murder.

He takes my silence as an answer. "Could you send a tray of chocolates and a bottle of pink champagne to the suite?"

I'm still full of cheesecake, and I've had plenty of alcohol, but I'm determined not to argue.

I swear Kalina's face falls. I have the feeling she wants to get rid of me, even though she told us about the specials. "Of course. I'll bring them up myself in a few minutes."

Logan leads me to the elevator. From the corner of my eye, I see one of the resident ghosts lounging in a chair. I also notice Kalina slaps down her gloves a little too hard, making Baldwin jump. As if it's a statement about goofing off, he hides the crossword book, adjusts his readers, and begins typing on the computer.

Did she know Sal, I wonder? Could she wield a garden trowel like a weapon?

The elevator dings, and the door panels slide open. "Kalina?" I call. "Where were you when Sal was killed?"

She glances around, looking slightly horrified, but no one pays attention to us. The few couples present are filing in and out of the area for the event.

Her husband, however, glances up and zeros in on me. "What kind of question is that?"

Kalina hurtles toward us, still watching for anyone who might be listening. "I'm sorry, but what are you insinuating?"

"You were at the desk that night, correct? You saw Victoria sneak a bottle of schnapps from the bar."

I point at the double doors farther down. There's a closed sign on them, but a staff member has been going in and out with trays of fancy drinks. I assume there's a bartender inside.

"Victoria did what?" Baldwin appears surprised, removing his glasses, then shoving them back on. He starts typing. "Did you add it to her room bill?"

"Of course I did," Kalina insists, but she sounds like she's covering. She rushes back to the desk and stills his hands with hers. I overhear her say quietly, "It's been taken care of. Would you be a dear and go see about that champagne? I'm not sure we have enough pink in stock."

He removes his readers. "I ordered a whole case for the Single Lady Fizzies."

"Baldwin." Her tone is one I've heard many times when Mama is warning me not to sass her. "Please go make sure there's an unopened bottle for Mr. Cross and Miss Fantome."

Baldwin, like me, knows better than to argue with that tone. He rises from the chair and passes us, as Logan holds the elevator doors open.

"I'll put you down for another night. The food and drinks will be delivered shortly," Kalina calls with a fake smile.

I take a couple of steps closer to her. "Did you know Sal?" Still holding the door, Logan reaches out and tries to tug me back.

Kalina smiles even sweeter now. "I'd never met him before Thursday. I sure hope Detective Jones finds the culprit and wraps this up quickly. This poor hotel has been through enough in its lifetime without the bad publicity this is bringing."

Logan's hand finally manages to grasp my arm, and I step in with him, thinking that the hotel is getting a great deal of business because of the fair, regardless of the crime. However,

I couldn't agree more that this old place has been through enough. It doesn't make sense for her to commit murder if she's truly worried about her bottom line.

Of course, crimes of passion are rarely logical.

As the doors close, I realize I haven't ruled out anyone nor discovered further evidence.

I'm back where I started.

## ❧ 20 ❧

U pstairs in the suite, I pace. "I need to start at the beginning and work through this again."

In good attorney fashion, Logan grabs a notebook and begins writing down the details, creating a timeline, and quizzing me about the different players and what their motivation could be as I talk.

My internet searches so far have been about Tallulah. Lowering myself into a cushy chair near the fireplace, I turn my attention to Sal and do one for him.

There's not much outside of the usual social media pages, but he's listed the places he attended school. The college catches my eye, so I try that in connection with his name and come across an article about a dress design contest he won there. I'm about to pass by the photo of him and the runners-up when a face that seems familiar stops me.

I zoom in. In the black and white picture, the woman isn't staring at the camera but at Sal. He holds up an award and trophy. Her hair is different, but I'm sure I recognize that profile.

Reading the article, I scan the names. "Aha!" I bolt to my feet. "You're not going to believe this."

Logan looks up from the doodles on his notepad. "What?"

I blow up the picture and turn it so he can see the screen. "Do you know who that is?"

"Sure, it's Victoria."

"They were both in this design contest in college. He won a scholarship and an internship to work with Tyrone Worthington."

Logan gives me a blank look. "Should I know who that is?"

"He's a famous bridal designer." I stare into the dark fireplace, thinking about the two young college students, and the repercussions of Sal besting her.

Logan flips to the page he started on her, adding the information. "What was the date?"

I check. "Two-thousand thirteen. Victoria came in fourth. There's some motive for you."

"Really? For murder?"

I bite my thumbnail. "That scholarship and internship may have changed the direction of her life. She wanted to be a wedding gown designer, and she ended up a bridal fair planner."

"That's a long time to wait to get revenge, and it seems kind of petty, don't you think?"

"Not at all. The fashion designer business is extremely cutthroat and hard to break into."

He waggles the pen between his finger and thumb. "But Sal didn't become a designer either. He worked for a bridal shop. He never created his own gowns, did he?"

"Maybe that's why he was so happy putting mine down." I sink into the chair once more. "He never made his dream come true, even after winning that opportunity. I had no idea."

"And you think Victoria killed him because of that?"

I sure wish Sal's ghost would visit so I could confirm the theory and get clarity on what was going on between them. "It's not proof, but it's more than what we had. I'm sure my dad would say people have killed for less. Maybe Victoria had a crush on Sal." I do another quick search. "Doesn't look like she's married, maybe never has been. He may have ruined her hopes for a career and turned her down for a relationship. A woman scorned and all that... Men should know better than to mess with us."

Logan reviews the notes and moves back and forth between sheets. "Penn mentioned Sal was going to report Victoria. Wonder what that was about?"

"Maybe he didn't like her flirting with him. He may have threatened to mention her behavior to Top Events' management, and she wanted to stop him."

"Sexual harassment?" He writes the word under Motive with a question mark. "Murdering him over that still seems extreme. Those cases are usually he said-she said, although typically, it's the other way around with the woman filing the complaint."

"True, but maybe he was threatening her to get her to stop. I mean, if he was never interested in her, and she was coming on to him, it's kind of sad, but knowing Sal, he *would* report it. What an ego boost for him."

"Not a super likable guy, was he?"

"Not with people he worked with. The brides all seemed to love him."

The chocolates and champagne arrive, but it's not Kalina who delivers them. It's a staff member. I'm guessing she did that on purpose so I couldn't question her further.

The candies are pretty, but they're not nearly as good as Queenie's. I only take a bite of a cherry topped one, and throw the rest away. Logan starts to pop the cork, but I stop him. "I need to keep a clear head."

Once again, I feel slightly guilty, as he sets the chilled bottle in the fridge, but I truly need to figure this out, and I'm a bit of a lightweight when it comes to liquor. "There's something we're missing, too many facts, not enough concrete evidence. I'm running out of time. If I could just solve either Tallulah's situation or Sal's murder, I'd feel a lot better."

"Who's Tallulah?"

"A ghost who haunts this place. She's the daughter of the original owners and she's... Never mind. Long story. Our most pressing issue is Sal."

Logan studies his notes in silence. I'm about to put forth another theory when a knock sounds on the door. We exchange a look.

"Who could that be?" I whisper. "We already received the chocolates and champagne."

He shrugs.

I tap the notepad and make a motion for him to stick it in the bedroom as I go to the door.

A good thing too, because the person on the other side is the last one I want to see right now.

Detective Jones stares at me through the crack. Tabby rubs against his legs. "Miss Fantome," he says, his voice dripping with his accent. "We need to talk."

## ❧ 21 ❧

"What do you want?" I keep the door partially closed. "I was just getting ready for bed."

He hooks his thumb in his belt loops. "I need to ask you a few more questions."

Logan's hand touches my shoulder as he peers over the top of my head. "About what?"

Jones appears slightly disgruntled that my attorney is here. His lips firm and a crease appears between his brows. "In regards to Mr. Luxton's death. We can either do it here, or I can take you down to the station. Your choice."

Some choice. He sounds too serious for my liking. I glance behind him to see my three suspects lined up along the wall. The Nottingham family peers down at all of us, serious and condescending.

Sherlock appears, floating near the onlookers. He seems agitated. Or perhaps excited. He keeps making obvious glances at the women as if indicting the killer.

But which one?

I point my chin at the eavesdroppers, pointedly staring at Victoria. "Are you interviewing them as well?"

Jones doesn't even glance over his shoulder. "I've already spoken to them, and you are the person I need to talk to now."

I peek at Sherlock. He nods. Approval?

While the suite is in no way mine, it feels like an invasion to let Jones in. Plus, I may decide to show him what I've discovered in the study in an effort to circumvent whatever the killer intended by planting—or hiding—it there. "I'll meet you at the other end of the hall in a minute. I need to run to the bathroom."

Tabby weaves in and out between his legs. She meows at me and looks up as if supporting my decision to speak with the detective. Sherlock also seems to endorse the decision, gliding in the direction of the study.

As Jones saunters off, the women follow. Logan draws me back and shuts the door. Tabby barely slides through, running over my foot before it closes. "As your lawyer, I highly recommend you say nothing."

"Actually, I think I need to tell him what we've unearthed."

"He hasn't arrested you yet, which means he's trying to trap you into saying something to incriminate yourself."

"I know that, but..."

"Ava, seriously, this is a bad idea."

Tabby scratches at the door and meows forlornly. "You'll be beside me to stop me from doing that, but I should tell him about the connection between Sal and Victoria. Also, there's something weird with Kalina."

Logan sighs audibly. "Refusing to say anything further until he has a warrant is a way to do that."

I rise on tiptoes and kiss him. "Those three witches out there are trying to hang me for this crime. Trust me, with a cop for a dad, I learned plenty of maneuvers to talk myself out of trouble. The best thing for me to do in this instance is throw suspicion back onto them. I can't do that if I stay silent."

He brushes a strand of hair from my shoulder. "I knew I couldn't talk you out of it, but I had to try."

I grab my phone. "I love you for it. Better grab the notebook."

Hand in hand, we move toward the study. Victoria, Christine, and Kalina are whispering in a huddle. They stop and watch me as Logan opens the door to usher me in.

I lean toward them and mutter as though I'm one of their gang. "I know who did it, and I'm going to prove it."

Not expecting this, they rear back as if I have a disease they're afraid to catch. The expressions on their faces could be fear. Either that, or they think I'm nuts.

The jury's out on that. As I disappear inside, I give them a Cheshire smile and a finger wave bye.

≪ 22 ≫

J ones has cleared one end of the large table and motions
for me to sit across from him. "Brought your watchdog,
I see."

Logan doesn't take offense and holds the seat out for me.
"Because she's smart."

The detective leans back, causing the heavy wooden chair
to groan under his weight. "That posse out there is quite
determined to pin this murder on you. Want to tell me why?"

I honestly wish I knew. I'm too anxious to sit and cruise
around the long table, trying not to worry my fingers. Sherlock has resumed his station by the fireplace. "Because one of
them—maybe all three—had a hand in it. They need a
scapegoat."

Tabby slips past me and under the table.

Surprisingly, Jones doesn't argue or seem confrontational.
He simply nods. "Got any evidence to support that?"

What I have is shaky at best, but I launch into what I've
pieced together. I grab several fancy fountain pens from a
reading table that holds an F. Scott Fitzgerald novel and position them under the yellowy light of the nearest banker's

lamp. Each represents a player in the situation, and I move them around as I walk him through a possible theory of what happened.

Quiet as a mouse, he listens and watches the writing utensils, his face devoid of expression. Logan adds a comment here and there, but otherwise, he also remains quiet and focused. Sherlock sits, pipe in hand, reading a book and appearing not to listen at all.

"Then there's this." Using my phone, I pull up the picture from the contest.

Jones' shoulders barely move in a shrug. "So?"

I relay the facts about Sal winning, and the possible consequences for Victoria. "There's a link between them. Victoria may have been jealous or angry. She might have been looking for revenge. Then there's a possibility she had a crush on him and never got over him." I tap the notepad where Logan wrote down the information about Victoria flirting with Sal. "A member of our group thinks she overheard Sal threatening to report her. Could be for sexual harassment."

"You think I don't know how to use an internet search engine?" Jones stares at me. "I already discovered that photo, and while your theory may be accurate, I still have no proof."

"But I—"

Logan touches my hand to silence me. "Detective, you know Ava didn't do it. You're not here to arrest her, so why don't you tell us why you *are* here."

The detective's massive arms uncross, and he runs a hand over his face as if weary. "A lot of strange things have occurred in this building. Unexplainable things."

I wasn't expecting that, and wonder if he knows about Tallulah and the baby. "Like what?"

"Like, I don't believe this is the first murder to occur on these grounds."

A cold cramp forms in my belly. Surely Emanuele wouldn't kill his grandson. But if not that, then what?

My wild imagination—thanks to too much stress and not enough sleep—wonders if Kalina and Baldwin have some sick enterprise going on the side. I'm almost afraid to ask. "There have been others?"

"My grandmother was a maid here in the late sixties. While most of the year was dead, summers were busy. Tallulah refused to hire extra help. Mammie Pauline was a hard worker, but she couldn't keep up with this huge place when it was crowded. They had dumb waiters in the kitchen, the laundry, a couple other locations. Most had been boarded up, unused. Mammie discovered one and knew it could come in handy—they didn't have an elevator then."

It looks original, I'm surprised. "I can't imagine trudging up and down three floors every day."

"Carrying food, laundry, bed linens. Her back never was right after she worked here. The elevator wasn't added until the nineties when the next owners bought it and turned it into a spa. Had to meet codes for handicapped guests."

He toys with the pens that represent Cathi and the photographer in my scenario. "Mammie found it hidden behind wallpaper in the barroom. She asked Miss Tallulah for permission to uncover it, and I guess Tallulah flew into a rage, according to her, ordering her to patch it up and never go near it again. But Mammie was curious as a cat. Sneaky as one, too." He eyes Tabby, now lounging in a chair next to him and purring. "She found bones in it. Always said they belonged to a child."

Logan rears back. "Bones?"

The earlier cold spreads, a heavy brick in my stomach now. I swallow. "Did she report it?"

"A black woman in the fifties, here in Georgia, with a

steady job and a half-crazy, white employer? Sure, she rushed right down to the police station."

His thick sarcasm fills the air. "She told you, though, when you became a cop."

His chin dips in acknowledgment. "Tallulah was long gone by then, but I was curious. Your daddy and I investigated. The owners back then cooperated, albeit reluctantly. When we opened up the space, it was empty. We assume Tallulah moved them."

I think of the cemetery and the simple square-cut stone. "Oh my," I say, the letters rearranging themselves in my mind, like drawings on a chalkboard. "Monroe, Romone. She named the baby after him."

Both Jones and Logan stare at me, questions brewing in their gazes.

"Come again," Jones says.

"There's a grave under the tree outside with only the name Monroe on it. I think it may have been Tallulah's baby."

Sherlock looks up and touches the side of his nose signifying I've hit the truth.

Jones narrows his eyes. He knows my reputation for being a ghost whisperer. He doesn't believe in such things, being all about logic and evidence he can see and touch.

"Maybe it was an accident," Logan offers. He's always seeking the most logical answer, too. "The child may have went in there on his own and died somehow."

"Guess we'll never know." Jones continues studying me. "But from the way Mammie described them, the child probably wasn't old enough to even crawl."

I feel sick. I need to believe it was as Logan said. "What does this have to do with Sal?"

His eyes dart around the room. He waves a finger. "This place has a lot of secret doors, passageways—hidden things such as those dumb waiters. Our killer may know of and have used more than one to assist him or her on Thursday night. I can get a warrant, but a search like that could take days, maybe weeks. There's over six thousand square feet. There are so many nooks and crannies, we could get lost ourselves. At the moment, I believe our culprit and the weapon are here inside this hotel, but I need an inside man, so to speak. Someone to bring me a piece of solid evidence to close this case before the fair is over tomorrow afternoon."

"You *have* the weapon," I remind him. "The shoe."

He leans forward, placing both elbows on the table. "This has not been released to the public yet. I want your word you won't share it with anyone."

Logan and I exchange a glance, then nod in unison. "We promise," I say.

"That is not the only weapon."

I point at a pen. "We know about the object that knocked Sal down. Something hard and metal, with a sharp edge to it that broke the skin."

"There is that, and I shared that information on purpose so those women might give up something, but they haven't. What I'm talking about is a different matter altogether. A cylindrical item with a sharp point caused the initial neck wound. Our murderer knocked Mr. Luxton out, then while he lay on the ground, took something like an ice pick, and stuck it into his neck." He motions at the corresponding placement on his own. "The heel was inserted in the puncture wound created by that cylindrical object afterward to try and disguise it."

I sit back at this news. "An ice pick? Like they might have in the bar?"

"The medical examiner almost missed it, thanks to the tearing caused by the end of the stiletto , but we believe so. The killer missed the jugular, but death would've been quick regardless. There should've been a healthy amount of splatter on the person who struck him."

"Did you search for an ice pick?" Logan asks.

"The owners claim they don't have one." He rubs his face again. "Whoever jabbed our victim had to be facing him, they would've been hit with blood, then took the time to shove a shoe heel into the wound as some sort of statement."

I pick up the pen, reenacting what must have happened, jabbing it down as if Sal is on the table. "The blood would have been on the killer's hands, her face..."

A nod from the detective. "Barring a confession, I need that weapon or a witness."

"You want Ava to do what, get it for you?" Logan glares at Jones when he doesn't argue. "You've got to be kidding."

Jones keeps his focus on me. "Think you're up for the task, Fantome?"

Ironic. Normally, the detective is railroading my family into situations where I have to fight him. "Am I up to doing your job for you? It's not like I haven't done it before."

A hint of a smile quirks his lips. "You've tried, I'll give you that. Since you think this killer may be attempting to frame you, I thought you might want a hand in bringing them to justice."

"It's too dangerous." Logan gives him a scorching rebuke. "Go get your search warrant."

I set down the pen and extend my hand to Jones. "Deal."

We shake.

"Ava," Logan says, my name a warning.

"I'll be fine. You'll be here to help me." To Jones, I add, "By the way, you better look under the table."

Jones releases my hand with a curious stare. "Why?"

I motion for him to lean down. Shifting his big body, he manages to do so.

Logan does, too, the three of us staring at the rocking

chair and shoe. Tabby jumps off to sit next to the chair. She paws at the shoe, and I snap my fingers at her. "Don't touch."

"Is that what I think it is?" Jones asks.

Sherlock chuckles. "He's quite shocked."

"Yep," I say. "The matching shoe to the bloody one left in Sal's throat."

We all rise, and he pulls out an evidence bag from his jacket. "I'll have it tested for prints and DNA. Anything else I should see?"

"You can't seriously put my client in this dangerous situation," Logan states.

"I like him," Sherlock says.

Jones disregards Logan's concern. "As Ava said, you'll be here to protect her. I'll be stationed about a mile down the road tonight. I'm dog-eared tired, but we're not letting this killer leave tomorrow and make us look like small-town hicks. Anything happens, text or call, I'll be here in minutes."

Logan shakes his head, still unhappy. I glance between the men. "Let's catch us a killer."

## 23

Jones leaves, making sure the other women see the shoe in the evidence bag. They clamber after him as he makes his way to the elevator.

"Aren't you arresting her?" Victoria's voice rankles my nerves.

Jones punches the button. The sound of the cables kicking in echoes down the hall. "Her alibi is tight."

"She claims she was chasing a cat," Christine practically yells. "No one saw her."

Jones looks up at the numbers above the door, completely unperturbed. "Actually, she was making out with her boyfriend in a broom closet next to the atrium."

All three women's heads snap to the right, glaring at Logan and me.

"She's lying." This from Victoria.

Jones shrugs. "I've got no solid evidence against her."

The doors open and he climbs inside. They shove in, continuing to berate him about my suspected guilt, their voices fading as it closes and the elevator descends.

Logan glances at me and shakes his head. "What's your plan?"

Honestly, I don't have one—yet. I look at Tabby. "Anything you want to tell me?" *Like who the killer is?* She blinks as if bored and says nothing. "I think I need to talk to my dad."

Back inside the suite, I dial his cell. Daddy picks up on the first ring. "Hi, sweetie, everything okay?"

I put him on speaker. "Remember that look you used on me growing up? When I was in trouble, and you wanted me to fess up to my crimes?"

He chuckles. "You never were a natural liar, but you still tried. Your mother would get so upset when she knew you were pulling her leg, but you'd never break with her."

Logan grins. I return it. "But I did every time with you. What's the secret? I mean, when you were on the force, you used that technique with suspects, I bet, right?"

"Sure, lots of times. People tend to talk too much when they're guilty. Most have sort of an internal button that, when pushed, makes them implicate themselves, and they can spill all kinds of secrets."

He pauses, and I hear Mama in the background, asking a question. "Be right there," he calls, then he lowers his voice to me. "Is this about the murder investigation?"

He knows me well. "You didn't teach that technique to Detective Jones, or if you did, it isn't working for him on this one."

"He has his own methods, and you should leave the police work to him."

I don't want to worry my father, and telling him I'm collaborating with his former partner on this isn't wise. "I'm trying to get a secret out of Logan."

I'm glad Daddy can't see my face, since he'd pick up on the whopper I'm telling now.

This seems to relieve his mind, though. He chuckles again. "You think he's going to pop the question?"

Logan's humor fades, and he drops his head and leans on the back of the plush sofa.

"Something like that." Guilt wells inside my chest. I push it aside. "So what's the trick?"

"Silence."

"I don't understand."

"People want to fill it. You tell them you know their secret and then you wait. In the case of a suspect, you pretend you already know *why* they did it. This is validating and sounds sympathetic, which always helps. Then you shut up, and you stare at them like you can see their truth written on their foreheads."

"That's it?" I've used the silent technique before and had fair results, but not in a life and death situation like this.

"Well, my pretty blue eyes might have helped." His laughter is contagious, making Logan and I both grin again. "Gotta run. Your mother has something planned. Happy Valentine's Day, sweetie. I hope you get what you want."

"Me too," I say. "Happy Valentine's Day, Daddy."

I disconnect and put my phone away. Logan grabs a flashlight and taps it against his palm.

"Afraid the electricity will go out? It's not storming."

He leads me to the door. "You're about to provoke a killer. Staring them down might get a confession, but it won't do any good if they try to stop you from revealing it."

Good point.

In the hall, Tabby is playing with one of the fancy pens, using her paw to smack it around on the floor runner. I retrieve it and stick it in my pocket. She meows, indignant.

I bring it back out and hold it up. It's heavy and cylindrical. It has a sharp point. *Nottingham Hotel* is written on the barrel in a vintage script. "I bet this is an original."

Logan eyes it, the overhead light glinting off the casing. "They don't make pens like that anymore."

I study the point. "Could easily puncture someone's throat, don't you think?"

The elevator doors open as if by magic. We give each other a look before stepping inside. Tabby follows. Logan takes the pen and examines it in more detail. "Definitely could break skin with enough force."

On the first floor, we pass Kalina, once more on duty at the desk. She glares at me suspiciously. "Is there something I can help you with?"

"The chocolates were delicious. We're just on our way to talk to Cathi. She's in room twelve, right?"

I actually have no idea if the girl is still here, but Kalina reveals she is.

"Six." She stands to keep an eye on us. Laughter filters out from the Sweetheart Saturday crowd in the dining area. "Why do you want her?"

"Because she stole my shoes."

I have no proof—it's simply an educated guess, but I'm taking Daddy's advice and pretending I know more than I do.

Halfway down the hall, I stop and pivot back to stare at her. "Plus, I'm pretty sure she knows who the killer is."

Kalina's face goes ashen. She glances at a couple exiting the ballroom. They hustle past and head for the lobby doors. "Shh," she hisses. "You're scaring the guests. Detective Jones said—"

"Yeah, I know. He's taking the shoe I found to be dusted for fingerprints and DNA. The funny thing is, Cathi was wearing them." Again, I'm throwing out a theory without any concrete evidence. "If she jabbed Sal in the throat with one, there'd be blood splatter on the other as well as the gown she wore. But...she was spotted over here"—I point—"with the photographer at the same time Sal died. Curious, don't you think?"

She's reluctantly come around the counter and edged closer. As the dining room noise fills the space between us, I let the question hang and see the wheels spinning in her brain. "So, she took off the shoes before she came out here to talk to Jason?"

Plausible. "She left them near the murder scene, and quite possibly saw who was around Sal at that moment." I spin once more to the door and knock.

"Who is it?" A man's gruff voice calls.

"I'm looking for Cathi. Is she in there?"

The door flies open a foot, and a bare-chested Jason with his hair mussed looks me over. "Where's the food?"

He's not much taller than I am. "Sorry, not room service."

I spot Cathi over his shoulder. She's trying to sneak into the bedroom, nothing but a blanket around her frame. I call over his shoulder. "Can I have my shoes back? I know you stole them—er, *borrowed*, I guess. No hard feelings, I won't press charges, but I need them."

Jason stares holes through me. "Hey, I know you. You're the gal that Christine hates."

Okay then.

"Watch it," Logan growls, tapping the flashlight in his palm.

My watchdog seems quite menacing, and Jason takes a step back. I make a mental note to reward Logan later.

"Look, Jason, I just want them back. If you and Cathi don't return them, I'll have no choice but to file a complaint with the police. Detective Jones will be returning with a warrant to search the hotel soon. You're going to appear highly suspicious if you have a dozen boxes of stolen shoes in this room, and who knows what else."

Cathi peeks out, her eyes wide. "I didn't steal nothing. I only wanted to try them on."

I give her an understanding smile, hiding my irritation. "I know you did, but now you've had your fun playing dress up," —I glance at Jason and his chest—"fantasizing about your wedding and honeymoon."

"Wedding?" Jason turns on her. "What is she talking about? You don't think...?"

He makes a disgusted noise, grabs his shirt from the floor, along with his camera bag. He shoves past me and Logan, leaving the door open. "I'm out of here."

"Noooo," Cathi calls running after him, nearly tripping. "Jason, don't leave!"

It's a scene worthy of a reality show as she chases him down the hall and into the lobby, clad only in the blanket.

Meanwhile, I motion to Logan and we enter the room. The boxes of my shoes are neatly stacked next to the mirror attached to a door. Several wedding gowns hang on hooks around the room and in the open closet.

"Oh, dear," Kalina says, having trailed in after us.

"You might want to make sure she didn't steal those as well." I point to the gowns.

Logan and I confiscate my boxes, clearly marked with Enchanted Events, and walk out.

I lead us to the ballroom. He flips on the lights and we stack the items on a table inside the booth. Flipping off lids, I'm checking that they're all accounted for when Christine bursts in.

Fire in her eyes, she marches across the floor, swinging her arms with determination, a mannequin appendage in one hand.

She raises it as she draws near. "How dare you threaten my sister!"

## 24

She stalks us, shaking the bare appendage at me. "You made her cry!"

Logan raises the flashlight in defense. I punch a couple buttons on my phone, turning on a recording app that I've found handy before, and stand my ground. "She stole my shoes, as well as various items from other vendors."

The plastic limb nearly touches my nose. "She may have tried them on, but she didn't steal them. She was going to return them tonight."

Logan slides slightly in front of me. "Lower the weapon."

Christine glances at the arm and registers his meaning. She drops it next to her side. "Oh. I was setting up a display for tomorrow in the lobby entrance. Sorry."

"Let's all take a deep breath." He points at the table. "We've recovered the missing shoes. You should go help Cathi return the other items."

"She's bawling like a baby because of you." She jabs the piece at me once more and flinches when Logan knocks it away.

Lowering it, she huffs. "She came running after Jason. Told me you made him break up with her."

"Your sister needs to..." I notice Kalina darting past the open doors, her furtive movements suggesting she hopes we won't see her. "I'll be back in a minute."

I skirt around Christine and rush out, leaving Logan arguing with her about Cathi's kleptomania. In the foyer, I catch Kalina going left toward the atrium.

Among the plants and flowers, couples mingle with the Saturday drink specials in hand. I search but she seems to have disappeared. Leaves brush my arms and legs as I walk around scanning the area.

Tallulah appears near a rubber tree ahead of me along the path that leads to the courtyard. She doesn't motion at me or say anything, but casts a glance over her shoulder as she floats away, a clear invitation to follow.

Winding around camellias, peace lilies, and exotic plants I don't know the names of, we come to a half-wall at the south end. She drifts into an alcove where a work station with clay pots and a bag of soil is located. A series of gardening hand tools hang above the bench.

Several half-dead ivy plants and two brown ferns sit on the floor near a door marked Exit, as if waiting to be taken out to their final resting place. The door is nearly hidden in the dim light, but a glimmer of illumination peaks through the side and beneath the crack. Someone has left it partially open, an outside glow from the moon and stars oozing through.

As I reach for the handle, Persephone materializes on my left. "Goodness, Ava. Pay attention. She's trying to show you something."

I glance back, letting Persephone's irritation roll off me. "I know Tallulah. It's Kalina."

"No." My guardian angel palms her forehead and sighs,

exasperated. "Look again."

Pivoting, I scan the space Tallulah's spectral body hovers near. I see her point at the lined-up items on the wall. A trowel—the one I used to fend her off, in fact—a cultivator, and a fork. "What about them?"

"Check closer." Persephone floats to the other side of the bench.

Both spirits stare at me, practically willing me to get it. "It's the trowel, isn't it?"

Persephone rolls her eyes and says to the ghost, "Told you she was slow on these things." Then to me, "Don't view what's there. Search for what's *missing*."

Ah, an empty hook, a bare space between two of the tools. "The murder weapon?"

"Hallelujah." Persephone throws her hands in the air.

"But what is it?"

Tallulah speaks. "A dibbler."

That means nothing to me. I need to brush up on my gardening knowledge, especially since Aunt Willa created a backyard garden that's worthy of a magazine spread. "Okay, so who's the killer?"

Tallulah glances at her feet, hovering several inches above the concrete floor. "I don't know."

I can't tell if her ghost is being truthful or not. "Why are you helping me?"

Her gaze rises slowly to meet mine. It's full of sadness, but also something else. "Because you're the only one who's ever been nice to me."

I glance at Persephone for confirmation. She winks and vanishes.

At least I have more to go on than I did. "Thank you," I tell Tallulah. "I'm going to help you, but I need to find the killer first, all right?"

Like Persephone, she withdraws from view.

I step outside. The night air is cold. Murky clouds have moved in and dance around the moon. It takes a moment for my eyes to adjust to the velvety gray blanket of night, only a few stars reflecting off the lake in the distance.

I notice a hulking maple casting a shadow over the end of the courtyard, the atrium's lights not reaching it. "Kalina?" I call softly.

Rustling comes from a plant beside the tree, a figure emerges. "Yes?" Her voice sounds as if she's attempting to sound chipper, as if I haven't just interrupted her break. "Can I help you?"

I catch the scent of cigarette smoke on the air. "Trying to quit?"

She steps closer, head down, and I hear a quiet sigh as she realizes it's me. "I did six months ago. This weekend has made me start again. You won't tell Baldwin?"

Not if she cooperates. "Where is the missing hand tool from the bench?"

"What?"

I cock my thumb toward the alcove. "The one next to the cultivator. Do you use it often?"

Even in the shadows, she's close enough now I can see her frown. "I didn't notice it was gone."

"A dibbler, right? What do you use it for?"

She looks away, toward the rolling hill sand lake. "Planting seeds. It creates a hole in the soil for you to drop them in. I don't grow things from seeds, so I never use it."

Truth or a well-rehearsed excuse? "But it came in handy when you murdered Sal."

"What?" She turns back toward me, her voice rising. "I had nothing to do with that and you know it. Besides, he was killed with a shoe."

"We both know that's not true, and now that I've identified the true murder weapon, having your husband find out you took up your old habit again is the least of your problems."

She takes a half-step toward me and points a finger. "You're certifiable, you know that? If you'll excuse me, you're making me nervous. I need to get back to my desk and the guests."

She brushes past, and I pivot to watch her grab the door. "Where is Baldwin? Guess I need to speak to him about what his wife's been up to."

This stops her, one palm on the handle. She grips it tight enough to turn her knuckles a whitish gray. The soft light from the interior atrium shows her face. She bites her bottom lip, working something over in her mind. "Look, I haven't been completely honest about what I saw that night."

Aha. Now we're getting somewhere.

I close the distance, hoping my recording app can pick up her lowered voice. "I know." I give her my dad's infamous stare. "Why don't you start at the beginning?"

## ❧ 25 ❧

"Are you okay?" She frowns at me. "You look like you're gonna be sick."

Obviously, my technique needs work. "I'm fine. What happened?"

"First, I don't know who killed that man, and I'm not pointing fingers, but..."

"But what?"

She shifts her weight and fiddles with the knob. "I saw Victoria come out of the bar and go to her room while the show was in progress. She returned a few moments later, frazzled, and said she stole some liquor."

Nothing I didn't already know. "Okay, so?"

"I think she switched trousers and put on a different suit jacket."

Victoria tends to wear the same outfit—a black skirt or pants and a white blouse with a black jacket on top.

"I was aggravated that she took the bottle—that's what she claimed, anyway—because we needed it for tonight's specials, and I didn't think to ask why she'd changed. I was more annoyed that she'd left Baldwin to wrap up the show."

"How did she get from the backstage where she was chasing Tabby to the bar without you seeing her?"

"Because I was out here," Kalina points to the maple.

She stares at me as if willing me to promise I won't tell. "Your secret is safe with me."

*For now.*

Satisfied, she nods. "There's something else."

"Go on."

"A hidden staging room connects the ballroom's backstage area and the bar. It's where the maids and servants used to prep carts and serving trays during big parties. Victoria might have found it and gone through there to get to the bar after... you know. It's a possibility, anyway. The thing is, I went to count the bottles the next day, but none were missing. Odd, don't you think?"

"Maybe you miscounted your inventory to begin with."

She shakes her head adamantly. "Trust me, I had Baldwin double-check the number when they were delivered. We don't have a lot of margin. We count pennies to remain open."

I think over the timeline in my head, and why Victoria might lie about the liquor and change her clothes. It's not obvious proof of misdeeds, but I would like clarification. "Where's she right now?"

Kalina shrugs. "Last I saw, she was in the dining room."

I can't exactly call Victoria out in public, and I don't want to confront her until I have more to go on. "Why didn't you tell Jones this?"

Exasperated, she throws her hands up. "Because I don't want anyone knowing I left the desk and went out for a smoke."

"Okay, okay. I get it." I motion for her to go in ahead of me and close the door as she passes the alcove.

She stops to look back. "What are you going to do?"

I hesitate, thinking it over. "I need a key to Victoria's room."

"Are you nuts? I can't let you trespass."

"Kalina, she could be the killer. Your lie—or withholding of the truth—could implicate you, as well."

Her eyes tear. Fear is a great motivator. While I might not have dad's technique down, I seem to have my own.

She turns on her heel, seeming to have made up her mind. Better to keep her secret than protect Victoria. "Follow me."

At the desk, she looks around to make sure no one is watching, then hands me a key.

As if I own the place, I march past people filing in and out of the dining room. I pause a moment to peer in. Sure enough, Victoria is sitting with another vendor, enjoying a drink.

At her door, I slide the key in the lock and sneak into her room.

## ❧ 26 ❧

I flick on the light. Tabby jets past my legs and I close the
door behind us.

An assortment of items from various booths are scattered
amongst her personal things. On the bed, a large suitcase is
open, half-folded clothes and toiletries nestled inside.

Is she packing to leave already?

Tabby jumps on the bed and paws at the suitcase. Her
meow rings in the small room. I shush her and notice a
collection of candlestick holders, guest books, hair accessories, ring pillows, and a flower girl basket crowded together
on the desk. A laptop is under the mess.

What is she doing with all these props?

I don't see any gowns or shoes like Cathi was hoarding,
but still, I wonder. Is Victoria helping herself to some of the
samples, or perhaps they were gifted to her?

Tabby meows again, drawing it out. I make my way to the
bed and the open suitcase, where she paws at the contents.

I was wrong—it's not clothing, but an assortment of
colored fabrics, like scarves. Shifting through them, I realize
some cover plastic bags containing more items.

What in the world? Does she have some sort of fetish for wedding supplies?

What I assumed were toiletries are actually miniature shampoo and soap samples from the destination vendors. The bottles have places for the bride and groom's wedding date to be stamped on them.

My hand knocks against one with something hard in it. When I shift the fabric aside, I see it's Victoria's metal document holder.

It's sealed in a plastic bag. I turn on the nightstand light and aim it toward the item before taking a photo with my phone. Then I send the picture to Jones, asking if I should open it and see if our murder weapon is contained inside.

Why would Victoria pick the dibbler to stab Sal with? While it's definitely an effective weapon, was our crime of passion premeditated? At least enough that she saw the garden tool and decided to use it to kill Sal? Or did she snag it in hopes of framing Kalina or someone else?

Tabby hops off and moves to the chair. While I wait for Jones to reply, I think about having a peek at the laptop. As I move the clutter aside, I see Victoria's backup clipboard.

The top page is filled with handwritten notes. Along with those are X's, checkmarks, highlights, and certain items are crossed off. Her to-do list is long. I flip that over to see what's underneath.

Vendor's names are listed in alphabetical order. Next to each is a handwritten monetary amount. Southern Bride has a question mark next to their name instead of a dollar sign. Enchanted Events isn't there at all.

My phone buzzes and I jump, expecting Jones. Instead it's Logan. *Where are you?*

*Room twelve.*

I snap a picture of the list, trying to figure out the

meaning of the numbers next to their names. Some range up into the thousands.

As I'm doing that, Jones finally replies. *Don't touch it. I'm on my way.*

I'm studying the written notes again when Victoria bursts in. "What do you think you're doing?"

Tabby comes to my side, tail up.

"What are you doing with all this stuff?" I point to the various samples that are still in obvious view. "You and Cathi should go into business together."

"How dare you break into my room." She points to the door. "Get out."

"They're gifts, aren't they?"

"Yes, so what?"

"What do you do with them? Resell them?"

Her jaw jumps as she clenches her teeth. "That's none of your business. I'm going to complain."

"Go ahead. I didn't break in." I hold up the key. "Besides you don't want everyone to know about your little scheme, do you?"

"You think you're so smart. What scheme? I work for an event management group and vendors gift me things. Big deal."

I lean over the desk and tap her clipboard. "What about the money? Are they offering you bribes, too?"

"Don't be ridiculous." She marches to me and grabs my arm. "Get out."

She attempts to shove me toward the door, but I plant my feet and jerk from her grip. "Why isn't Enchanted on here?"

Frustrated, she glares at me. "Because you're a trouble-maker and I don't like you."

"Wow, that stings." I run a hand over a guestbook on the desk. "My guess is, you knew I wouldn't pony up. But for what? What do the vendors get if they give you items from their inventory and top it off with money?"

"They're not bribes. You wouldn't understand."

"Try me, or I'm going to report you to your employer. I bet they'd be very interested to learn about your side enterprise."

She studies me, as if deciding just how much of a trouble-maker I really am. "For your information, most of the people work on commission. The more they sell at these conventions, the more lucrative their bottom line. Occasionally, they supply me with samples. That allows me quality assurance—I check that their products are up to our standards. In turn, I make sure they get better slots for their booths, and that ensures the brides are happy."

She moves and fingers one of the tall candlestick holders. The overhead light glints off the metal as she evaluates it. Hastily, I fumble with my phone, attempting to turn on the recording app while she isn't looking.

"What do you do with all of them? Surely you don't keep them for yourself."

Logan bangs on the door. "Ava. What's going on?"

"I'm having a chat with Victoria." I call back, easing toward the exit. All she has to do is step away from the desk and block me.

Seeing my intention, she does exactly that. "What does it matter? They get what they want and we all benefit."

"You wanted to be a designer. Why didn't you pursue that?"

Her lips tweak in a snarky smile. "Someone's been talking to Sal."

"I did my homework. You can find anything online, you know. Were you crushing on him?"

Her smile goes flat. "What a loser. He totally wasted his

opportunity. If I'd won that scholarship..." She looks at the items in the room.

"You wouldn't be stuck here running bridal events. You'd be designing and selling your own gowns."

She caresses the candlestick again. "Your gowns are beautiful. You have a good eye for design. I could have created gorgeous ones, too, if only Sal hadn't gotten in my way."

"He was on to your scam here, wasn't he?" I wave a hand at the space.

"A troublemaker like you. He didn't understand why I accept the gifts and the money, but then, he never really understood me at all. I'm *helping* the vendors. You see that, right?"

"What did you do with the murder weapon?"

"What?" Her eyes dart to the suitcase and back. It's so quick, I almost miss it. "I have no idea what you're talking about."

I stare her down for a long, charged pause, hoping my dad's trick will work. She narrows her eyes at me, but says nothing.

Out in the hall, Logan calls, "Ava? Let me in."

I attempt to move past Victoria but she stands firm. "You're not going anywhere," she says quietly.

"I'd like to, but I can't," I answer him.

Logan yells down the hall at Kalina. "I need you to open this!"

"Think you're pretty smart, don't you?" Victoria's gaze zeroes in on me. "Sal thought he was as well."

*And look what happened to him.* She doesn't finish the thought but the threat is in her eyes.

"You asked for a bribe from Southern Bride—from him, specifically—and he said no, I take it?"

"He stole that internship from me. The least he could do is pad my retirement."

Distantly, I hear Kalina reply to Logan. "There are only two keys. Victoria has one and Ava the other."

"So you're taking bribes, both in sample products and money from the big vendors," I clarify, hoping the app is getting all this.

Victoria can't seem to keep the smile off her face now. "I think of it as an effective marketing strategy for them."

"Sal was going to report you to the head office, so you killed him."

"It was his own fault." Her grip tightens on the candle-stick. "He was going to ruin me once again. I had to stop him."

Before I can breathe, she grabs Tabby by the back of the neck. "Tell your boyfriend you're fine. We're just chatting. You'll meet him upstairs in a bit."

Tabby screeches, dangling by her scruff. "Or what?" I dare her.

"What do you think?" She gives the feline a shake. "I'll kill the cat."

I purse my lips. "You could try, but I don't think it will work, unless she's on her last life."

Tabby glares at me and swipes a claw through the air.

The candlestick rises over Tabby's head. "Tell him."

"Fine," I mutter. Raising my voice, I inform Logan, "Everything's good. We're talking weddings. I'll be upstairs in a few minutes and we can resume where we left off earlier."

A long pause. Logan seems confused as his muffled voice comes through the door. "Are you sure?"

"Yep. It's all good."

There's murmuring between him and Kalina, and then the sound of retreating footsteps.

Victoria drops Tabby, who darts under the bed. She then taps one end of the candlestick in her palm, reminding me of Logan with his flashlight.

Not waiting for her to attack, I launch myself around her to get to the exit.

My shoe catches on a crumpled edge of a throw rug. I lose my balance, knocking into the side of the bed and then flailing into the wall.

Victoria advances, candlestick aloft.

I throw up my hand to ward off the anticipated blow. "Now you're going to kill me, too?"

"I'm certainly not going to allow you to ruin everything!"

"Logan and Kalina know I'm in here."

She lowers her arm, but only to pull back the rug and throw it aside. "Not if I throw you in the cellar."

"What?"

She slips her fingers between two wooden boards where a notch is missing. A square of flooring rises to reveal a hidden room below. "I'll say you left, and I don't know what happened to you."

I scramble to my feet, my ankle screaming in pain. "You've lost it, Victoria. The jig is up."

She uses the candlestick to point at the cellar. "I'll escape before they ever find your body. There's a secret exit to the stables down there. I'll be drinking Mai Tais on the beach and you'll be one more ghost in this haunted establishment."

Fun thought, that. "You have no idea how terrifying that actually is for me."

She advances and I push off, ignoring my unstable ankle. Sidestepping her swing, I reach for the door handle, but the candlestick connects with my back, pain erupting between my shoulder blades.

I fall to my knees. She claws at my hair and grips a chunk before jerking me away from the door and onto my back. I see the candlestick arc in the air and come down toward my head.

Tabby's high-pitched screeching *meeeeowwwww* echoes in the room. Victoria screams.

I grab the weapon in her grasp and yank. Off balance, she tumbles to the floor next to me, releasing my hair. I scramble to wrench the item free and smack her in the arm. Tabby defends me once more, leaping from the bed and landing on Victoria's face.

As Victoria shrieks and tries to remove the cat, I crawl for the door. "Help!"

As I reach it, she grabs me and hauls me backward. I elbow her in the ribs, then pivot to punch her. Poor Tabby lies limp near the bed.

Victoria stumbles. I kick her in the stomach for good measure.

As she gasps and doubles over, finally sinking to the ground and not moving, I throw open the door.

Logan is there. I fall into his arms.

## 🦋 27 🦋

Sunday dawns bright and clear. The morning is packed with the last of our attendees finalizing dates, times, and products they want for their upcoming weddings. I feel a cheerful relief to what has been hanging over the whole event due to Sal's death, although I'm sore from my encounter with Victoria.

Kalina does an excellent job taking over as coordinator, ensuring that all have a successful conclusion, and lining up another for next year, back here at the hotel.

"Isn't it great?" she asks, as she carries a yearly planner. "Vendors are already putting deposits down! We'll be able to fix up more of the rooms so everyone who registers has the option to stay here during the fair."

"It's a great place for this." I hand her my card. "You can put us down, too."

Rosie raises her eyes from her laptop where she's itemizing a bride's order. "We'll need a larger booth next year, and at least three rooms reserved for that weekend. Top billing for the runway, and complimentary child care."

"I'll make a note."

Mama has brought several city council members and is showing them around. They stop next to Kalina. "We have a few ideas we'd like to run by you for a Fourth of July festival. The Thornhollow Chamber and Council have to okay the details, but I think this would be the perfect place for it."

As the two walk off, chattering and making plans, Detective Jones arrives and pulls me aside. "Victoria confessed after three hours of interrogation," he tells me. "You were right. The dibbler was used to kill Sal, and she planned to sneak out last night. I've uncovered an illegal network she was tied to. They steal wedding supplies and resell them on the internet. Also found an evidence trail of the bribes she's been taking and depositing in an offshore account. She's made quite a lot of money over the years. Apparently, she was about to change her identity and live on an island."

"So I did good, huh? Made you look competent."

It seems to pain him to agree. "You have a bit of your dad in you. A nose for this stuff."

"And you appreciate me putting my life on the line to catch her, right? Leading to you putting a gang of thieves out of business, too. Wow, pretty impressive, if I do say so myself."

He reaches out and pats my shoulder. "Don't get a big head, Fantome. You did well. I'll buy you a coffee one of these days."

After he leaves, I meet with Reverend Stout and a friend of his who's a Catholic priest. I ask the priest to perform a ceremony at the gravesite of Tallulah's child.

I don't share the details, and he seems okay with that. Tabby sits next to the marker as he blesses the soul of the child, asking the angels to escort the child to heaven. My ancestor is no worse for her efforts to stop Victoria, having recovered from the blow dealt her.

I see Tallulah peeking out from behind the tree. She gives

me a sad smile. "Monroe was stillborn," she tells me as the priest reads a verse from his Bible. "I went a little mad when Mama couldn't make him cry. I'd lost too much blood giving birth and ended up out of it for days. When I finally came to and had my wits about me, she told me she'd taken care of him. We never spoke of it after that, and until that maid discovered the bones, I'd assumed she'd buried him in an unmarked grave."

I'm relieved to know the child didn't suffer.

"I never told the father, your friend's daddy. I never saw him again after he left this place, and I didn't know what I'd say to him. It was one night, our secret love affair, and I thought the baby would be a reminder to me about that connection. I had so much grief after Monroe died, I couldn't function right. Mama did everything she could to help my mind, but it was off. Guess I'm sort of glad Abe found love with someone else and had a happy life."

She fades after the ceremony is complete.

The men leave, and Gloria catches up with me. "I have good news," she announces. "I contacted an investor friend who is interested in helping Baldwin and Kalina fully restore the hotel. She's part of a local historic property committee, and since the building and acreage are relatively unchanged since it was built, she feels it will qualify for acceptance into their Historic Landmarks Program. That's sure to bring tourists who love historical markers from all over the country."

Tallulah appears behind Gloria, and so does Gloria's father. They don't say anything to me or each other, but I see them exchange a look. Something passes between them; they're coming to an understanding.

"That's amazing." I put an arm around her. "Say, do you have a minute? We need to finish our conversation about your dad."

"Of course, *ma cherie.*" She draws something from her pocket. "Here is my favorite picture of him. Doesn't he look like the man in that old photo you found?"

He does indeed. "Handsome guy."

We stroll past the courtyard and stand looking at the rolling hills while I tell her everything I know. The sun reflects on the lake, turning it into dozens of diamonds.

She sheds tears over Tallulah and the baby, and states she had no idea about her father's life before he married her mom.

"You know I speak to those who've passed over sometimes, right?"

She nods. "Like your dear auntie."

"Tallulah and your father have both been here the whole weekend. I think she's found some peace now, so I'm delighted you've taken an interest in this place and are going to help it thrive again."

Tallulah nods. "All is forgiven," she says. I know this is directed at him rather than us.

Gloria looks around as though searching for the ghosts. Not seeing them, she takes my hand, and we begin walking back. "I'm overwhelmed thinking about all of it. Thank you for telling me."

The midday sun is warm on our faces, and some of the early spring bushes are blooming. "It really is a spectacular place," she says, stopping to smell a flowering vine growing along the courtyard's entrance.

Tabby lies on a warm patio stone, purring. Kalina bursts from the atrium and rushes to us. "You're not going to believe this."

After this weekend, there isn't much that would surprise me. "What happened?"

She sees the distressed look on my face and waves it away. "The news is out about the event, the murder, Victoria, and everything. There's a *movie* producer who just called and offered to shoot a documentary here. The local papers are also asking for feature stories."

Gloria claps. "Excellent news."

I smile. "Very cool."

"That's not all. Are you familiar with the theater group a few towns over who do the mystery dinners? They want to host one here next month."

She squeals with delight and Gloria and I laugh. Through the window, I see Tallulah waving at me, as if to say goodbye. She's smiling, too.

Gloria tells Kalina about her investor as I observe the ghost. Tabby rises to her feet and watches along with me as a glowing lighted doorway appears in front of Tallulah. She hesitates for a moment, still leery at what waits for her on the other side. When she glances at me, I nod, offering her encouragement.

Others float toward the portal, their phantasmal figures flying by and through her, as though they've been waiting for this chance. The woman I saw the night of the runway show stops and stands next to her. Now that I see them next to each other, I recognize their similarities. Apparently, Tallulah's mother, Mary Mae, has been hanging around a long time as well.

Gloria's father appears beside them, and in his arms is a baby. Tallulah's face lights up and she reaches for the child.

Abe pats her shoulder then walks into the light. Tallulah squeezes her son in a hug and he coos and laughs. The sound reaches my ears and makes me happy.

A glance back and she mouths the words, "Thank you." Her mother gives me a serene smile.

I nod, and witness their forms disappearing into the light. Tabby meows.

Sherlock appears near the cat. "Well done, Ava."

Persephone materializes at my side. "They're all at peace now."

"Are you okay?" Kalina asks. She and Gloria are staring at me.

*Oops.* Must have missed something. "I'm so happy for you," I tell Kalina. "It's time this place had new life."

## ❧ 28 ❧

After the never-ending weekend, I'm exhausted but happy by the time Logan and I arrive at The Wedding Chapel that evening.

I perk up when I find it decorated with hearts, a full meal ready and waiting from Queenie, and Arthur and Lancelot happy to see me. Even the gargoyles on each side of the steps and the knocker seem relieved I'm home.

"Too quiet around here," the knocker says as Logan unlocks the door.

Luckily, he can't hear the inanimate objects.

Tabby doesn't even glance at the boys as she heads upstairs. I'm not the only one who's tired.

Logan leads me out to the garden, the food artfully arranged on the gazebo's table. Moxley is lounging near the water fountain and barks a greeting. Red and pink roses, greenery and baby's breath fill a vase. Fairy lights twinkle from the railings and the arch.

Brax has brought over the B&B's fire pit, which burns brightly and warms the air. The late evening sun splashes across the scene, tiny sparks jumping up, and the scent of burning wood filling my nose.

Logan has secured a new bottle of champagne and pops the cork. Music comes from the back porch, a few birds singing along before they nestle down for the night.

I'm finally able to let go of everything that happened and simply sit and enjoy the moment. I've been dreaming of it for a long, long time.

"Life is never dull with you," he says, pouring me a glass.

"You can still back out, you know. I won't hold you to your earlier proposal."

He grins. "You're not getting rid of me that easily."

Where there's food, there are cats. Tabby has revived and joins us on the lawn. Arthur and Lancelot prowl around, pretending not to be interested, but keeping an eye under the table in case crumbs drop. Moxley doesn't roam, but he's every bit as zeroed in as they are. It feels right to have them here, witnessing what I anticipate is about to happen.

Of course, Logan makes me wait for it, insisting we eat while it's hot.

The meal is delicious and I'm stuffed by the end. I sense my aunt here, and I suspect my mother and Queenie are hovering near their phones, waiting for me to call and tell them about the proposal. Because, of course, they already know.

Every once in a while, I feel someone's eyes on us. I glance at the bed and breakfast, but never see Brax or Rhys. Doesn't mean they aren't watching.

As we finish with Queenie's famous rum bread pudding— a favorite of mine that I've managed to get Logan hooked on —he clears his throat and raises his glass in a toast. "To us."

Simple and sweet. I gently clink mine against his. "To us. You'll always have my heart, Logan."

Tabby jumps on his lap, pawing at the inside pocket of his

blazer. He pats her head, deposits her back on the ground, and removes the small blue box.

As he rises to come to my side, I reach across and stop him. "You don't have to get down on your knee. You don't even have to ask me again. You know the answer."

He laughs and drops to one knee next to me. "We're doing this my way this time."

The diamond must be three carats. I'm scared I'll lose it, but then I hear my aunt say, "No, you won't. You'll love it and care for it, just like you will him."

Tears sneak into my eyes. Logan looks so gallant and handsome in the firelight. "Ava Fantome, will you marry me?"

Any guy who'll put up with all my quirks and weirdness with seeing spirits and talking to cats is one in a million. I lean over and kiss him. "Yes, please."

He returns it, taking his time to thoroughly steal my breath. As he takes the beautiful ring from the box, slipping it onto my finger, I wiggle my hand so it catches the light. "Wow."

"If you don't like it, we can exchange it."

"It's perfect." And it is. "I can't believe this is happening."

Persephone pops in, eyeing the remnants of our dinner. "About time."

Ignoring her, I hug Logan around the neck. Tabby jumps on his empty chair and meows. Aunt Willa appears in the distance. She blows me a smooch, her big smile the last thing I see before she vanishes once more.

Mama and Queenie don't even wait for the text. They've been hiding inside the whole time, and startle me when they rush out the back door squealing and clapping. Moxley gets to his feet and barks.

Each embraces me, then Logan. Brax and Rhys come over, and we go through the whole hugging thing again.

Inside, the celebration continues with my dad showing

up. "You take care of my baby, y'hear?" he tells Logan and Logan promises to do so.

"Daddy," I chastise.

He hugs me. "I know, I know. You can take care of yourself. Congratulations, Ava."

I'm filled with hope for the future for all of us, getting on with our lives and creating happy ones in this small town in Georgia.

After the others leave, Logan and I settle on the couch. I waggle my finger some more, admiring my new diamond. "It's so big."

"Too much?" he asks.

"Never."

He smiles and kisses the end of my nose. "I figure once we're married, I'll move in here, if that's okay. It's definitely larger than my apartment. Can the cats handle Moxley?"

"Of course. Maybe we can blow out the wall between two of the upstairs bedrooms and make a suite."

"The hotel is rubbing off on you."

"It sure is grand. Haunted, but cool."

He rubs my hand with his thumb. "I'll keep my office, of course, and I can use the apartment for poker nights."

I slide a glance his way. "You don't have poker nights."

"I assume there may be times when you need to talk to ghosts and stuff, or when you go to the Thorny Toad to offer readings."

I sit up. "Who said anything about performing at the Toad?"

"Brax said..."

"Brax?" I shake my head. "What am I going to do with that man? I'm not taking up where Aunt Willa left off, rest assured."

"Okay, but there may be instances when you need a break from me."

"Do you even know how to play poker?"

"Don't you?"

I laugh and kiss him, and he tickles my side. "We have a lot to learn about each other," I say. "By the way, ghosts don't come on a regular schedule, so you'll have to get used to that."

"They're not gonna watch me when I'm in the shower or anything, are they?"

"No guarantees, but I think I'll probably be the only one doing that."

We talk and laugh. Logan insists I need rest, and I don't argue when he gets up to leave.

Standing in one of the front display windows, I watch as he makes it across the street with his dog. Holding Moxley, he blows a kiss to me before going inside.

Feeling content and sleepy, I turn and startle when Persephone is standing there. "You did a good thing helping Tallulah and her child. You stepped up to the challenge. I'm proud of you."

"Thanks." I hold my tongue from mentioning that Sherlock was more help than she was.

"Congratulations on the engagement. Did you set a date?"

"I'm thinking maybe June first— I've always wanted to get married then. The gardens will be beautiful out back, and I'd like us to do it here."

"You're going to be busy between now and then."

At first, I assume she's referring to the wedding preparations. Three months isn't long.

Then, I remember: this is Persephone. She's talking about ghosts. "Oh, no. Now what?"

"Reverend Stout has a ghost hitchhiker from the hotel. One looking for vengeance."

I pass by her, heading for the stairs, ready for a long soak and a good eight hours in my own bed. "Well, he'll have to wait. I'm booked."

"Ava..." Her tone holds a warning.

Sherlock pops in. "Give the girl a break, Seph. She's had a rough one."

Persephone rolls her eyes. "Why are you still hanging around?"

He adjusts his hat. "I find you quite intriguing."

If a guardian angel can blush, mine does. "I am, aren't I?"

"How about we leave Ava alone and go have some fun?"

He offers her his arm and she reluctantly slips hers through it. "What kind?"

"Thank you," I say to Sherlock. Tabby rushes past me. "Goodnight, Persephone."

She says, "Goodnight, spirit walker," and the two disappear, Persephone's laughter ringing in my ears.

I SURE HOPE YOU ENJOYED THIS STORY AND I'D LOVE TO hear from you!

Sign up for my Cozy Clues Mystery Newsletter and be the FIRST to learn about new releases, sales, behind-the-scenes trivia about the book characters, pictures of my pets, and links to insightful and often hilarious *From the Cauldron With Godfrey blog*

Ready for more ghostly adventures with Ava and the gang?
**Vows & Vengeance is coming soon!**
**Be sure to sign up for the newsletter to get the preorder links as soon as they're available!**

Read on for a sneak peek at If the Cursed Shoe Fits, Once Upon A Witch, Book 1...

## IF THE CURSED SHOE FITS,
## CHAPTER 1

"Cinder!"

My sister's screech jolts me upright from my prone position under the workroom sink and I smack my forehead on the steel basin. "Ouch!"

A follow-up shriek and the sound of shattering glass in the showroom has me muttering to myself and wiping my wet hands on a rag. "Coming," I call, scuttling out from under the pipes. A bucket, half filled with dirty water and hair from the drainpipe, along with numerous fittings and tools, are scattered around my legs.

"It's one of your mice," Belle calls. "They're loose again!"

Technically, they aren't *my* mice, but I tend to have an assortment of small critters who take to me, like McAlister, my pigmy hedgehog. The orphaned mice babies are now bigger than he is and strong enough to return to the woods where I found them last month. I brought them in, always a sucker for hurt or abandoned animals, and my sister, Ruby, helped feed and nurture them like their missing mother would have if she were still around. Now, it's time for us return them to the forest behind our home.

Sliding the bucket filled with a tangle of Zelle's coppery hair out of the way, I get to my feet. McAlister, on the countertop, stirs from his nap. He's nocturnal but still loves to be in the thick of things around the shop.

Zelle doesn't wash her hair in this sink, and I suspect the mice have been busy building nests with it, especially since they're constantly escaping their enclosure.

In the showroom, I find Belle standing on a stool behind the cash register, a book in hand, as usual. Zelle, the sister who dropped a glass candle, is half sitting, half teetering on the edge of a display table, her weight threatening to topple it and a dozen stacked soap bars to the floor. Her outstretched legs wave in the air. "It ran behind the Magical Forest display!"

Rapunzel, known as Zelle, and Belle, are fraternal twins. Although they're not identical, they resemble each other enough that people who don't know them sometimes mix them up. Today, Zelle's spiky hair has pink tips on the ends and she's turned her twin's, a platinum blond.

Wiping a strand of hair from my forehead, I check behind the display. This reveals nothing more than dust and a cobweb. I mentally note we're low on Midsummer Night's Dream candles, the shelf they're housed on in the antique display cabinet nearly bare.

I turn to my younger sisters, "He's gone. You can get down."

Neither moves, scanning the shop floor with their matching brown eyes. "Where'd he go?" Zelle asks, suspiciously eyeing a nearby table of our sparkling Unicorn candles.

"Probably back to the workroom and the nest of hair you left in the drain."

Her feet hit the floor and glass crunches under her boots. "My hair?"

Since her locks grow at an astronomical rate, she shaves her head each morning. The hair regrows down to the floor by nightfall.

She touches the spikes already growing out from her morning routine, the signature pink tips part of her magick. "I haven't done anything in there in days, and I certainly haven't left any hair behind."

One of the goals I have for this year is growing our family business, the Enchanted Candle & Soap Company. Sales are thriving for our handmade, small-batch soaps and candles, especially online, and we're ready to add a full line of body care products. But a building expansion costs money. Money we don't have.

The upside is that a bigger showroom, workspace, and storage area will allow Belle and Zelle to up their hours, maybe even come on full-time, which Ruby and I could sorely use. As it is, the twins have to hold extra jobs in town to help pay our bills and keep our nearly two-hundred-year-old home from falling down around us. Belle works next door at the bookstore; Zelle is a hairstylist at Kit Kat Hair and Nails, specializing in events such as weddings.

In Story Cove, there are lots of weddings, along with parties of every make and kind, and good ol' Southern gatherings. Funerals and wakes, even simple Sunday dinners, are turned into big occasions.

"I know," I admit to her. "It's the—"

At that moment, I see a flash of gray from the corner of my eye. My hand shoots out in that direction. "Freeze!"

The mouse—half in, half out of the fall display near the cash register—stops dead in his tracks but squeaks loud enough to raise the hair on the back of my neck. I use my magick to keep him frozen as I scoop up his tiny body and look him in the eyes. "You've been a very bad little mouse. I know you're feeling your oats and are ready to get back into the forest, so we'll round up your brothers and sisters today and take a little journey, okay?"

His eyes convey more than his diminutive body could, even if it wasn't paralyzed. I allow my magick to roll back enough so he can move his head. His whiskers twitch as we stare nose to nose at each other, but I sense he understands my words and is relieved to return to the area where he was born.

My cellphone jingles in my back pocket, a chime to alert me to an incoming email. I take the little wiggler and hold him close as I pull it out. Zelle goes to grab a broom and dustpan to sweep up the glass candle, and Belle slides off her stool.

"Who's that?" she asks.

As I peruse the short message, I cringe. "One of those guys from the dating app. CuddlyBear59. Jeez, who makes this stuff up?"

"You got a match?" She hustles to my side to lean over my shoulder and read it. "An invitation to go to the ball?" She nearly squeals with glee. It currently seems to be her goal in life to set me up with someone.

"That's a big fat no."

She dances away, as though she has a partner waltzing her around the shop floor. "Tiffany Starling! Isn't it romantic? I can't believe someone so famous has moved to town, and is throwing a ball at her mansion. It's all for a good cause, too. She's helping the local theater with a silent auction fundraiser since they're going to perform the stage production of *The Glass Slippers*. The lead actress, Bonnie, will be wearing the original shoes during the play!"

I've heard Belle and Ruby chattering about this the past few days, but I've ignored most of it. "That's nice," I say offhandedly, "but I'm not going, and I really wish you hadn't put me on Fairytale Love. It's embarrassing. Not one of the guys who's sent me an email is someone I would date. Not even if they were the last guy on earth."

Consternation burns in Belle's eyes and she stops her pretend dancing. "Couldn't you try, Cinder? Fairytale Love has made over a million successful matches worldwide so far, and they're growing every day. Give at least one guy a chance, please?"

Dating in Story Cove is no fairytale, let me tell you. Finding my Prince Charming and a happily-ever-after is about as likely as Belle going a day without reading a book, or Zelle not walking around with pink hair.

Glancing at the email again, I notice the signature. "Jason Bonners. CuddlyBear59 is the meat market guy?" Another cringe. "Sorry, no." I make a face, thinking of what he does as a butcher. "Yuck."

"You refuse to date everybody," she argues, the exasperation in her voice grating on my nerves. "You need to get out more."

Zelle returns, shooting me a smirk, but at least she doesn't jump in on the conversation. She sweeps up the broken glass and chunks of candle and I reply to the email with a, "thanks, no thanks" message.

I pocket the phone and pet the mouse. "I'm too busy here and working on the building expansion. I don't have time for a boyfriend, so let's put that on hold for now, okay?"

Belle ignores me and goes to the front door to flip the sign over. It's almost 9 a.m. and time to open. With one hand she shoos me off. "Go take care of your mouse."

"You'll remove my profile from the dating site app?"

"Later," she replies.

Our shop cat, Savannah, has another renegade mouse trapped by the tail under a furry white paw when I return to the back room. The Angora gives me a bored look with her mismatched colored eyes as I retrieve the tiny gray baby, and I thank her for not eating him. A yawn and a stretch before she goes to the old cookie jar we keep handy and begs for a treat.

"You're spoiled," I tell her, depositing the mice in a shoe box. She purrs as I give her a crunchy fish-shaped treat. She meows for a second, after inhaling that one, but I stand my ground and ignore her pleading attempts, nearly having to stuff my ears with cotton because of her loud, incessant meowing.

After McAlister and I round up the rest of the mouse family, I'm carrying the shoebox to the back door when Ruby enters.

I'm the oldest of the Sherwood sisters, then Ruby, followed by the twins. My sister has the darkest hair of all of us, but shares my fair looks and freckles.

She's dressed in her signature red cape, even though the September day is warming nicely, and carries a basket of fresh eggs. "Hey, the van is making a weird ticking noise again." Undoing the cape's ties, she shrugs it off. "I had to walk through the forest to Nonni and Poppi's this morning. Not that I mind the walk on such a beautiful day, but do you think you could look at it?"

Our delivery van needs a tune-up, and probably a new timing belt. More expenses, and more of my time. "I'll work on it as soon as I can."

"Want me to scramble up eggs for your breakfast?"

"I'm relocating the mice back to the forest, but I haven't had any coffee yet and I'd kill for one of your mushroom omelets."

"You got it." She peeks in the container and wishes the little critters well before McAlister and I exit with them.

In the bird-song filled woods, fallen leaves crunch under foot. The air is clean and crisp and I cast a magick spell on the mice to keep them from becoming food for larger animals.

I'm a softy at heart, and I can't stand the idea of them dying. I know it's part of nature, but they're orphans, like my sisters and I, and I wish them well as they scamper off into the burrow that was their original home.

The mouse who scared Zelle and Belle gives me another nose twitch and lifts a paw as if to say 'thank you.' I return the wave and amble back to our stately gothic home on Main Street.

The sprawling two bottom floors and a huge attic belonged to our fourth great-grandmother in the early 1800s. What began as a single-level dwelling for her family, grew when she started the company in her thirties after her husband died. She raised their six kids on her own.

Through generations of women on my mom's side, the soap and candle products have proved to always be in demand, and continue to support our family. We stick by Grandma Eunice's rules and put a little magick into every bar of soap, every candle. Now, with our lotions, body butters, serums, and loose tea and spices, we're taking Enchanted to a whole new level. We're still limited, however, with space and money for ingredients.

After I've had my omelet and coffee, I gather my things from the drain cleaning. Belle rushes to me in the workroom. "There's someone here to see you," she says, adding with a wink, "he's really cute."

My non-existent dating life is going to be the highlight of her day, no matter what I do.

I put McAlister in his cage. "Who is it?"

She leans closer and lowers her voice in a conspiratorial whisper. "It's Tiffany's son!"

"Tiffany?"

"Tiffany Starling! Honestly, Cinder, weren't you listening

earlier?"

I shrug, grabbing my pipe wrench, still damp from the morning's work. I need to clean my tools, toss out the slimy water, and make sure the drain pipe doesn't leak. Then it's on to the van. "Can't you wait on him?"

"He said he needs to speak directly to you."

Sighing, I stare at her, searching for the lie. She's trying to set me up with a guy, and will go to any length to do so. But there's no subterfuge in her gaze, only happy excitement.

Wiping my hands, I follow her out, pocketing the wrench in my worn tool belt. Zelle is redoing the display she disrupted earlier, and Savannah has taken up residence in a patch of sunlight on the floor. Belle's Pekingese, Jayne Eyre, sniffs at the pant leg of a guy about my age, standing in a shaft of the same bright sunlight coming through the front display window.

He's tall, wearing an expensive tweed jacket and dark slacks, his wheat blond hair casually tousled. A lock falls into his eyes as he examines one of the charcoal soap bars in our Blackbeard line of male soap and beard products.

"This is Cinder," Belle announces, and he turns from the display on the antique table with a big smile.

"Nice to meet you." He extends a hand, a pair of sapphire blue eyes making me catch my breath. "I hope I'm not bothering you,"—he glances at the tool belt—"but Mother wanted me to speak to you specifically. Something about a refill of peppermint lotion—body butter, I think she called it? You made a tin of it for her. She swears it reduces the swelling in her feet, and she needs to wear those famous shoes of hers this weekend. She needs a refill."

I hear the words, but can't seem to process them, his stunning eyes making my brain short-circuit. The air catches in my sternum and seems as frozen as the mouse was earlier.

He looks at me somewhat expectantly, and it takes great

effort to make my brain cells function again. When his gaze travels to the tool belt once more, I feel a flush of heat spreading up my neck. I gingerly touch the wrench and then point a thumb over my shoulder to the workroom. "I, uh... had to fix a pipe."

"I see. It appears you're a woman of many talents."

I'm praying I don't have grease on my face.

"Yes, well..."

Peppermint Pigs is the name I've been toying with for my latest creation, a foot cream borne of my own need for it, as well as Nonni's. She has terrible swelling in her aging feet. I keep adding magick to my portion, hoping to shrink my giant ones.

So far, it refuses to reduce my size 10s, but I do have soft skin.

Belle and Ruby love the name, Zelle doesn't. The salve is made with beeswax and honey, along with peppermint and vanilla, and is specifically for soothing tired feet. I haven't added it to our line-up yet since it's still in the beta testing phase, and I simply don't have time to create dozens of tins of it.

Ideas I have plenty of. Time and money? Not so much.

I remember the woman who came in two weeks ago complaining about her feet. I knew right off the bat she wasn't native to Story Cove, but I had no idea she was the famous actress who recently moved to town. "That's your mother?" I stammer. "Tiffany Starling?"

He's still holding out a hand and Belle clears her throat, startling me out of my awkwardness. "Sorry," I say, reaching to take it. "I didn't realize who she was. I'm so glad my potion —um, body butter—worked."

The warmth and solidity of his hand makes me not want to let go. "You didn't recognize her?" He gives a chuckle. "Don't tell her that. Her ego would take it hard."

I still haven't released his hand and a silly grin breaks over my face. "It's our secret. Nice to meet you...I didn't catch your name."

A bemused expression crosses his face at my apparent ignorance about his family. "Henri Finch Starling. Friends call me Finn."

*Finn.* Nice. Everything about him is really nice.

"She told me this place had something special about it. Straight out of a children's storybook, she said." He glances around. "She was right. Is it on the register?"

"Register?"

He releases my hand. Reluctantly, I let him. "For historical homes?"

Probably should be, but making repairs to the old place or expanding it would have to meet their strict guidelines—and cost even more. "Afraid not."

"She's a beauty." He winks and my breath catches again. "I can see you're taking good care of her."

Trying to at least. I need several thousand dollars to get the bats out of the attic and update the electrical.

*Someday.* "I'm sorry I don't have any of the lotion your mom wants on hand at the moment. I'll have to make a fresh batch and deliver it later today."

Mentally, I add one more thing to my to-do list.

"That would be great." His grin broadens and he reaches inside his jacket, withdrawing a square ivory envelope, and handing it to me. "Mother would like to invite you to our fundraiser and ball this weekend."

I can feel Belle nearly squeal with excitement behind me. Even Zelle comes to attention. "Thank you, but's not necessary. I'm happy to make up the foot cream for your mother. It's no big deal."

His smile falls. "We'll pay for the lotion and delivery. This isn't in exchange for that."

"Oh, no, I understand. It's just...dancing isn't my thing."

He slowly returns the invitation to his pocket, his brows drawing down. "Sorry to hear that. You might still enjoy it, even if you don't want to dance. There's music and food, and the silent auction of my mother's memorabilia from the film."

I attempt to look interested, but I haven't even seen the movie. "I appreciate the offer, but—"

"Just think about it okay? Maybe I'll see you later. You know where we live right? On the hill?"

In Story Cove, that particular hill is referred to as Millionaires Row. Ms. Starling purchased Myth Manor, if memory of Belle's chattering about it serves.

"We know," she states from behind the counter. She's finishing up with a woman who's buying several candles from our Charming Crystals line, and eavesdropping on our conversation at the same time.

He nods at me, waves at Belle. "Again, nice to meet you. I hope to see you soon."

The customer exits on his heels, and Belle nearly grabs and shakes me, she's so frustrated. "I can't believe you didn't accept that invitation."

Zelle shakes her head. "Honestly, Cinder, I can't either. He's handsome, rich, and look how awesome he is, coming down here to get lotion for his mom's feet."

Handsome, rich, and nice...I'm not sure why I'm running away from that, but all I can do is shrug. "We only just met him," I say, thinking I should push Belle at him since she's so enamored with his mom and her movie.

He's perfect for her, and maybe if she had a boyfriend, she'd leave me alone.

With that idea in mind, I head back to work.

**Read the rest now!**

172

# READY FOR MORE MAGICK?

**Don't miss the next exciting adventure!** Sign up for Nyx's Cozy Clues Mystery Newsletter.

**And check out these magical stories!**

## Sister Witches Of Raven Falls Mystery Series

*Of Potions and Portents*
*Of Curses and Charms*
*Of Stars and Spells*
*Of Spirits and Superstition*

## Confessions of a Closet Medium Cozy Mystery Series
*Pumpkins & Poltergeists*
*Magic & Mistletoe*
*Hearts & Haunts*

## Once Upon a Witch Cozy Mystery Series
If the Cursed Shoe Fits (Cinder)

Beastly Book of Spells (Belle)
Poisoned Apple Potion (Snow)
Red Hot Wolfie (Ruby) 2021
Hexed Hair Day (Rapunzel) 2021

# ABOUT THE AUTHOR

USA Today Bestselling Author Nyx Halliwell is a writer from the South who grew up on TV shows like Buffy the Vampire Slayer and Charmed. She loves writing magical stories as much as she loves baking and crafting. She believes cats really can talk, but don't tell her three rescue puppies that.

She enjoys binge-watching mystery shows with her hubby and reading all types of stories involving magic and animals.

Connect with Nyx today and see pictures of her pets, be the first to know about new books and sales, and find out when Godfrey, the talking cat, has a new blog post! Receive a FREE copy of the Whitethorne Book of Spells and Recipes by signing up for her newsletter http://eepurl.com/gwKHB9

# CONNECT WITH NYX TODAY!

Website: nyxhalliwell.com

Email: nyxhalliwellauthor@gmail.com
Bookbub https://www.bookbub.com/profile/nyx-halliwell
Amazon amazon.com/author/nyxhalliwell
Facebook: https://www.facebook.com/NyxHalliwellAuthor/

Sign up for Nyx's Cozy Clues Mystery Newsletter and be the FIRST to learn about new releases, sales, behind-the-scenes trivia about the book characters, pictures of Nyx's pets, and links to insightful and often hilarious *From the Cauldron With Godfrey blog*!

# DEAR READER

I hope you enjoyed this story! If you did, and would be so kind, would you leave a review on Goodreads and your favorite book retailer? I would REALLY appreciate it!

A review lets hundreds, if not thousands, of potential readers know what you enjoyed about the book, and helps them make wise buying choices. It's the best word-of-mouth around.

The review doesn't have to be anything long! Pretend you're telling a friend about the story. Pick out one or more characters, scenes, or dialogue that made you smile, laugh, or warmed your heart, and tell them about it. Just a few sentences is perfect!

And if you're interested in crystals, psychic readings, energy healing, astrology, or past lives, please visit https://crystalswithmisty.com/ to find out more about how these all-natural, fun services can help you live a calmer, healthier life!

Blessed be,

Nyx 🤍

Printed in the USA
CPSIA information can be obtained
at www.ICGtesting.com
LVHW012317181223
766854LV00053B/1580